2 —

5

DOGFIGHT

and Other Stories

Michael Knight

DOGFIGHT

and Other Stories

GROVE PRESS
New York

First published in 1998 by Plume, an imprint of Dutton NAL,
a member of Penguin Putnam Inc.

Printed in the United States of America

FIRST GROVE PRESS EDITION

ISBN-10: 0-8021-4330-X
ISBN-13: 978-0-8021-4330-3

Grove Press
an imprint of Grove/Atlantic, Inc.
841 Broadway
New York, NY 10003

Distributed by Publishers Group West
www.groveatlantic.com

07 08 09 10 11 12 10 9 8 7 6 5 4 3 2 1

For My Parents

Contents

Smash & Grab   1

Now You See Her   14

Dogfight   31

Gerald's Monkey   50

Sleeping with My Dog   68

Amelia Earhart's Coat   82

A Bad Man, So Pretty   97

The Man Who Went Out for Cigarettes   118

Sundays   126

Tenant   141

Smash & Grab

At the last house on the left, the one with no security system sign staked on the lawn, no dog in the backyard, Cashdollar elbowed out a pane of glass in the kitchen door and reached through to unlock it from the inside. Though he was 99 percent certain that the house was empty (he'd watched the owners leave himself), he paused a moment just across the threshold, listened carefully, heard nothing. Satisfied, he padded through an archway into the dining room, where he found a chest of silverware and emptied its contents into the pillowcase he'd brought. He was headed down the hall, looking for the master bedroom, hoping that, in the rush to make some New Year's Eve soiree, the lady of the house had left her jewelry in plain sight, when he saw a flash of white and his head was snapped back on his neck, the bones in his face suddenly aflame. He wobbled, dropped to his knees. Then a girlish grunt and another burst of pain and all he knew was darkness.

He came to with his wrists and ankles bound with duct tape to the arms and legs of a ladder-back chair. His cheeks throbbed. His nose felt huge with ache. Opposite him, in an identical chair, a teenage girl was blowing lightly on the fingers of her left hand. There was a porcelain toilet tank lid, flecked with blood, across her lap. On it was arrayed a pair of cuticle scissors, a bottle of clear polish, cotton balls, and a nail file. The girl glanced up at him now, and he would have sworn she was pleased to find him awake.

"How's your face?" she said.

She was long-limbed, lean but not skinny, wearing a T-shirt with the words *Saint Bridget's Volleyball* across the front in pastel plaids. Her hair was pulled into pigtails. She wore flannel boxers and pink wool socks.

"It hurts like hell." His nostrils were plugged with blood, his voice buzzing like bad wiring in his head.

The girl did a sympathetic wince.

"I thought no one was home," he said.

"I guess you cased the house?" she said. "Is that the word—*cased?*"

Cashdollar nodded and she gave him a look, like she was sorry for spoiling his plans.

"I'm at boarding school. I just flew in this afternoon."

"I didn't see a light," he said.

"I keep foil over the windows," she said. "I need total darkness when I sleep. There's weather stripping under the door and everything."

"Have you called the police?"

"Right after I knocked you out. You scared me so bad I practically just shouted my address into the phone and hung up." She giggled a little at herself. "I was afraid you'd wake up and kill me. That's why the tape. I'll call again if they aren't here soon." This last she delivered as if she regretted having to make him wait. She waggled her fingers at him. "I was on my left pinky when I heard the window break."

Cashdollar estimated at least ten minutes for the girl to drag him down the hall and truss him up, which meant that the police would be arriving momentarily. He had robbed houses in seven states, had surprised his share of home owners, but he'd never once had a run-in with the law. He was too fast on his feet for that, strictly smash and grab, never got greedy, never resorted to violence. Neither, however, had a teenage girl ever bashed him unconscious with a toilet lid and duct taped him to a chair.

"This boarding school," he said. "They don't send you home for Christmas."

"I do Christmas with my mom," she said.

Cashdollar waited a moment for her to elaborate but she was quiet and he wondered if he hadn't hit on the beginnings of an angle here, wondered if he had time enough to work it. When it was clear that she wasn't going to continue, he prompted her.

"Divorce is hard," he said.

The girl shrugged. "Everybody's divorced."

"So the woman I saw before . . ." He let the words trail off into a question.

"My father's girlfriend," she said. "One of." She rolled her eyes. "My dad—last of the big-time swingers."

"Do you like her?" he said. "Is she nice?"

"I hardly know her. She's a nurse. She works for him." She waved a hand before her face as if swiping at an insect. "I think it's tacky if you want to know the truth."

They were in the dining room, though Cashdollar hadn't bothered to take it in when he was loading up the silverware. He saw crown molding. He saw paintings on the walls, dogs and dead birds done in oils, expensive but without resale value. This was a doctor's house, he thought. It made him angry that he'd misread the presence of the woman, angrier even than the fact that he'd let himself get caught. He was thirty-six years old. That seemed to him just then like a long time to be alive.

"I'm surprised you don't have a date," he said. "Pretty girl like you home alone on New Year's Eve."

He had his doubts about flattery—the girl seemed too sharp for that—but she took his remark in stride.

"Like I said, I just got in today and I'm away at school most of the year. Plus, I spend more time with my mother in California than my father so I don't really know anybody here."

"What's your name?" he said.

The girl hesitated. "I'm not sure I should tell you that."

"I just figured if you told me your name and I told you mine then you'd know somebody here."

"I don't think so," she said.

Cashdollar closed his eyes. He was glad that he wasn't wearing some kind of burglar costume—the black sweat suit, the ski mask. He felt less obvious in street clothes. Tonight, he'd chosen a hunter green coat, a navy turtleneck, khaki pants, and boat shoes. He didn't bother wearing gloves. He wasn't so scary-looking this way, he thought, and when he asked the question that was on his mind, it might seem like one regular person asking a favor of another.

"Listen, I'm just going to come right out and say this, okay. I'm wondering what are the chances you'd consider letting me go?" The girl opened her mouth but Cashdollar pressed ahead before she could refuse and she settled back into her chair to let him finish. "Because the police will be here soon and I don't want to go to prison and I promise, if you let me, I'll leave the way I came in and vanish from your life forever."

The girl was quiet for a moment, her face patient and composed, as if waiting to be sure he'd said his piece. He could hear the refrigerator humming in the kitchen. A moth plinked against the chandelier over their heads. He wondered if it hadn't slipped in through the broken pane. The girl capped the bottle of nail polish, lifted the toilet lid from her lap without disturbing the contents, and set it on the floor beside her chair.

"I'm sorry," she said. "I really am but you did break into the house and you put my father's silverware in your pillowcase and I'm sure you would have taken other things if I hadn't hit you on the head. If you want, I'll tell the police that you've been very nice, but I don't think it's right for me to let you go."

In spite—or because—of her genial demeanor, Cashdollar was beginning to feel like his heart was on the blink; it felt as thick and rubbery as a hot water bottle in his chest. He held his breath and strained against his bonds, hard enough to hop his chair, once, twice, but the tape held fast. He sat there, panting.

The girl said, "Let me ask you something. Let's say I was asleep or watching TV or whatever and I didn't hear the window break. Let's say you saw me first—what would you have done?"

He didn't have to think about his reply.

"I would have turned around and left the house. I've never hurt anyone in my whole life."

The girl stared at him for a long moment, then dropped her eyes, fanned her fingers, studied her handiwork. She didn't look altogether pleased. To the backs of her hands, she said, "I believe you."

As if to punctuate her sentence, the doorbell rang, followed by four sharp knocks, announcing the arrival of the police.

While he waited, Cashdollar thought about prison. The possibility of incarceration loomed forever on the periphery of his life but he'd never allowed himself to waste a lot of time considering the specifics. He told himself that at least he wasn't leaving anyone behind, wasn't ruining anyone else's life, though even as he filled his head with reassurances, he understood that they were false and his pulse was roaring in his ears, his lungs constricting. He remembered this one break-in down in Pensacola when some sound he made (a rusty hinge? a creaking floorboard?) startled the owner of the house from sleep. The bedroom was dark and the man couldn't see Cashdollar standing at the door. "Violet?" he said. "Is that you, Vi?" There was such sadness, such longing in his voice that Cashdollar knew Violet was never coming back. He pitied the man, of course, but at the same time, he felt as if he were watching him through a window, felt outside the world looking in rather than in the middle of things with the world pressing down around him. The man rolled over, mumbled his way back to sleep, and Cashdollar crept out of the house feeling sorry for himself. He hadn't thought about that man in years. Now, he could hear voices in the next room but he couldn't make out what they were saying. It struck him that they were taking too long and he wondered if this wasn't what people meant when they described time bogging down at desperate moments.

Then the girl rounded the corner into the dining room trailing a pair of uniformed police officers, the first a white guy, straight out of central casting, big and pudgy, his tunic crumpled into his slacks, his belt slung low under his belly, the second a black woman, small with broad shoulders, her hair twisted into braids under her cap. "My friend"—the girl paused, shot a significant look at Cashdollar— "Patrick, surprised him in the dining room and the burglar hit him with the toilet thingy and taped him up. Patrick, these are Officers Hildebran and Pruitt." She tipped her head right, then left, to indicate the man and the woman respectively.

Officer Pruitt circled around behind Cashdollar's chair.

"What was the burglar doing with a toilet lid?"

"That's a mystery," the girl said.

"Why haven't you cut him loose?"

"We didn't know what to do for sure," the girl said. "He didn't seem to be hurt too bad and we didn't want to disturb the crime scene. On TV, they always make a big deal out of leaving everything just so."

"I see," said Officer Pruitt, exactly as if she didn't see at all. "And you did your nails to pass the time?" She pointed at the manicure paraphernalia.

The girl made a goofy, self-deprecating face, all eyebrows and lips, twirled her finger in the air beside her ear.

Officer Hildebran wandered over to the window. Without facing the room, he said, "I'll be completely honest with you, Miss Schnell—"

"Daphne," the girl said and Cashdollar had the sense that her interjection was meant for him.

Officer Hildebran turned, smiled. "I'll be honest, Daphne, we sometimes recover some of the stolen property but—"

"He didn't take anything," the girl said.

Officer Hildebran raised his eyebrows. "No?"

"He must have panicked," Daphne said.

Cashdollar wondered what had become of his pillowcase, figured it was still in the hall where the girl had ambushed him, hoped the police didn't decide to poke around back there. Officer Pruitt crouched at his knees to take a closer look at the duct tape.

"You all right?" she said.

He nodded, cleared his throat.

"Where'd the tape come from?"

"I don't know," he said. "I was out cold."

"Regardless," Officer Hildebran was saying to Daphne, "unless there's a reliable eyewitness—"

Officer Pruitt sighed. "There is an eyewitness." She raised her eyes, regarded Cashdollar's battered face.

"Oh," Officer Hildebran said. "Right. You think you could pick him out of a lineup?"

"It all happened pretty fast," Cashdollar said.

And so it went, as strange and vivid as a fever dream, their questions, his answers, their questions, Daphne's answers—he supposed that she was not the kind of girl likely to arouse suspicion, not the kind of girl people were inclined to disbelieve—until the police were satisfied, more or less. They seemed placated by the fact that Cashdollar's injuries weren't severe and that nothing had actually been stolen. Officer Pruitt cut the tape with a utility knife and Cashdollar walked them to the door like he was welcome in this house. He invented contact information, assured them that he'd be down in the morning to look at mug shots. He didn't know what had changed Daphne's mind and, watching the police make their way down the sidewalk and out of his life, he didn't care. He shut the door and said, "Is Daphne your real name?" He was just turning to face her when she clubbed him with the toilet lid again.

Once more, Cashdollar woke in the ladder-back chair, wrists and ankles bound, but this time Daphne was seated cross-legged on the floor, leaned back, her weight on her hands. He saw her as if through a haze, as if looking through a smeary lens, noticed her long neck, the smooth skin on the insides of her thighs.

"Yes," Daphne said.

"What?"

"Yes, my name is Daphne."

"Oh," he said.

His skull felt full of sand.

"I'm sorry for conking you again," she said. "I don't know what happened. I mean, it was such a snap decision to lie to the police and then that woman cut the tape and I realized I don't know the first thing about you and I freaked." She paused. "What's your name?" she said.

Cashdollar felt as if he was being lowered back into himself from a great height, gradually remembering how it was to live in his body. Before he was fully aware of what he was saying, he'd given her an honest answer.

"Leonard," he said.

Daphne laughed. "I wasn't expecting that," she said. "I didn't think anybody named anybody Leonard anymore."

"I'm much older than you."

"You're not so old. What are you, forty?"

"Thirty-six."

Daphne said, "Oops."

"I think I have a concussion," Cashdollar said.

Daphne wrinkled her nose apologetically, pushed to her feet and brushed her hands together. "Be right back," she said. She ducked into the kitchen, returned with a highball glass, which she held under his chin. He smelled scotch, let her bring it to his mouth. It tasted expensive.

"Better?" Daphne said.

Cashdollar didn't answer. He'd been inclined to feel grateful but hadn't the vaguest idea where this was going now. She sat on the floor and he watched her sip from the glass. She made a retching face, shuddered, regrouped.

"At school one time, I drank two entire bottles of Robitussin cough syrup. I hallucinated that my Klimt poster was coming to life. It was very sexual. My roommate called the paramedics."

"Is that right?" Cashdollar said.

"My father was in Aruba when it happened," she said. "He was with an AMA rep named Farina Hoyle. I mean, what kind of a name is Farina Hoyle? He left her there and flew all the way back to make sure I was all right."

"That's nice, I guess," Cashdollar said.

Daphne nodded and smiled, half-sly, half–something else. Cashdollar couldn't put his finger on what he was seeing in her face. "It isn't true," she said. "Farina Hoyle's true. Aruba's true."

"What are you going to do with me?" Cashdollar said.

Daphne peered into the glass.

"I don't know," she said.

They were quiet for a minute. Daphne swirled the whiskey. Cashdollar's back itched and he rubbed it on the chair. When Daphne saw what he was doing, she moved behind the chair to scratch it for him and he tipped forward to give her better access. Her touch raised goose bumps, made his skin jump like horseflesh.

"Are you married?" she said.

He told her, "No."

"Divorced?"

He shook his head. Her hand went still between his shoulder blades. He heard her teeth click on the glass.

"You poor thing," she said. "Haven't you ever been in love?"

"I think you should cut me loose," Cashdollar said.

Daphne came around the chair and sat on his knee, draped her arm over his shoulder.

"How often do you do this? Rob houses, I mean."

"I do it when I need the money," he said.

"When was the last time?" Her face was close enough that he could smell the liquor on her breath.

"A while ago," he said. "Could I have another sip of that?" She helped him with the glass. He felt the scotch behind his eyes. The truth was he'd done an apartment house just last week, waited at the door for somebody to buzz him up, then broke the locks on the places where no one was home. Just now, however, he didn't see the percentage in the truth. He said, "I only ever do rich people and I give half my take to Jerry's Kids."

Daphne socked him in the chest.

"Ha, ha," she said.

"Isn't that what you want to hear?" he said. "Right? You're looking for a reason to let me go?"

"I don't know," she said.

He shrugged. "Who's to say it isn't true?"

"Jerry's Kids," she said.

She was smiling and he smiled back. He couldn't help liking this girl. He liked that she was smart and that she wasn't too afraid of him. He liked that she had the guts to bullshit the police.

"Ha, ha," he said.

Daphne knocked back the last of the scotch, then skated her socks over the hardwood floor, headed for the window.

"Do you have a car?" she said, parting the curtains. "I don't see a car."

"I'm around the block," he said.

"What do you drive?"

"Honda Civic."

Daphne raised her eyebrows.

"It's inconspicuous," he said.

She skated back over to his chair and slipped her hand into his pocket and rooted for his keys. Cashdollar flinched. There were only two keys on the ring, his car and his apartment. For some reason, this embarrassed him.

"It really is a Honda," Daphne said.

There was a grandfather clock in the corner but it had died at half past eight who knew how long ago and his watch was out of sight beneath the duct tape and Cashdollar was beginning to worry about the time. He guessed Daphne had been gone for twenty minutes, figured he was safe till after midnight, figured her father and his lady friend would at least ring in the New Year before calling it a night. He put the hour around 11:00 but he couldn't be sure and for all he knew, Daphne was out there joyriding in his car and you couldn't tell what might happen at a party on New Year's Eve. Somebody might get angry. Somebody might have too much to drink. Somebody might be so crushed with love they couldn't wait another minute to get home. He went on thinking like this until he heard what sounded like a garage door rumbling open and his mind went blank and every ounce of his perception was funneled down into his ears. For a minute, he heard nothing—he wasn't going to mistake silence for safety a second time—then a door opened in the kitchen and Daphne breezed into the room.

"Took me a while to find your car," she said.

She had changed clothes for her foray into the world. Now, she was wearing an electric blue parka with fur inside the hood, white leggings, and knee-high alpine boots.

"What time is it?" he said.

But she passed through without stopping, disappeared into the next room.

"You need to let me go," he said.

When she reappeared, she was carrying a stereo speaker, her back arched under its weight. He watched her go into the kitchen. She returned a minute later, empty-handed, breathing hard.

"I should've started small," she said.

He looked at her. "I don't understand."

"It's a good thing you've got a hatchback."

For the next half hour, she shuttled between the house and the garage, bearing valuables each trip, first the rest of the stereo, then the TV and the VCR, then his pillowcase of silverware, then an armload of expensive-looking suits, and on and on until Cashdollar was certain that his car would hold no more. Still she kept it up. Barbells, golf clubs, a calfskin luggage set. A pair of antique pistols. A dusty classical guitar. A baseball signed by someone dead and famous. With each passing minute, Cashdollar could feel his stomach tightening and it was all he could do to keep his mouth shut but he had the sense that he should leave her be, that this didn't have anything to do with him. He pictured his little Honda bulging with the accumulated property of another man's life, flashed to his apartment in his mind: unmade bed, lawn chairs in the living room, coffee mug in the sink. He made a point of never holding on to anything anybody else might want to steal. There was not a single thing in his apartment that it would hurt to lose, nothing he couldn't live without. Daphne swung back into the room, looking frazzled and exhausted, her face glazed with perspiration.

"There." She huffed at a wisp of hair that had fallen across her eyes.

"You're crazy," Cashdollar said.

Daphne dismissed him with a wave.

"You're out of touch," she said. "I'm your average sophomore."

"What'll you tell the cops?"

"I like Stockholm Syndrome but I think they're more likely to believe you made me lie under threat of death." She took the parka off, draped it on a chair, lifted the hem of her sweatshirt to wipe her face—exposing her belly, the curve of her ribs—pressed it first against her right eye, then her left, as if dabbing tears.

"I'll get the scissors," Daphne said.

She went out again, came back again. The tape fell away like something dead. Cashdollar rubbed his wrists a second, pushed to his feet and they stood there looking at each other. Her eyes, he decided, were the color of a jade pendant he had stolen years ago. That pendant pawned for $700. It flicked through his mind that he should kiss her and that she would let him but he restrained himself. He had no business kissing teenage girls. Then, as if she could read his thoughts, Daphne slapped him across the face. Cashdollar palmed his cheek, blinked the sting away, watched her doing a girlish bob and weave, her thumbs tucked inside her fists.

"Let me have it," she said.

"Quit," he said.

"Wimp," she said. "I dropped you twice."

"I'm gone," he said.

Right then, she poked him in the nose. It wouldn't have hurt so much if she hadn't already hit him with the toilet lid but as it was, his eyes watered up, his vision filled with tiny sparkles. Without thinking, he balled his hand and punched her in the mouth, not too hard, a reflex, just enough to sit her down, but right away he felt sick at what he'd done. He held his palms out, like he was trying to stop traffic.

"I didn't mean that," he said. "That was an accident. I've never hit a girl. I've never hurt anyone in my life."

Daphne touched her bottom lip, smudging her fingertip with blood.

"This will break his heart," she said.

She smiled at Cashdollar and he could see blood in the spaces between her teeth. The sight of her dizzied him with sadness. He thought how closely linked were love and pain. Daphne extended a hand, limp-wristed, ladylike. Her nails were perfect.

"Now tape me to the chair," she said.

Now You See Her

Xavier tells me he is upstairs doing his homework, but I know that he is watching our new neighbor. Grace Poole lives in the town house just across a narrow alley from our own. I was taking trash to the alley on Monday when I noticed my son at our second-story window, his face close enough to the glass to breathe mist onto it. I followed his eyes across the way, and there was Grace Poole, standing naked in her kitchen, sipping from a coffee mug. She gave no indication that she saw me or that she saw my son, perfectly still, entranced, huffing brief ghosts of longing against the pane. Today is Friday, and I've been watching her myself ever since. I have the benefit of binoculars.

I believe that I should be angry at him, should sneak up the stairs, right now, kick his door open, and demand to know what he thinks he's doing. But I'm not angry. X—he has started calling himself X— is thirteen. I remember thirteen and being full of that strange water, drawn and released by the sight of a woman, tides and moon. X was in such a hurry to get to his window after school that he didn't even stop to wonder why his old man is home this early in the day. How can I be mad at him? Grace is, at this moment, swimming closer to me through the binocular lenses.

I have often thought about having the talk with my son, about what I would tell him. The birds and the bees, the facts of life. For a man who spent his days talking, my own father, a professor of literature, was surprisingly inarticulate. He was maroon-faced and shifty and read me a poem about love. He tried to establish a connection.

"Do you know what I mean, Byron?" he said. "You know already, right?"

"Sure. I've got it covered," I said. I was twelve and only four years from discovering that I had nothing at all covered.

X has never seemed the right age for that sort of talk. Nine and ten, still too much a boy. Eleven, the year his mother died. My wife, Sarah. I couldn't get my head around anything that year, except the fact that she was gone. Her absence was everywhere. Dust on the piano keys. Dirty dishes in the sink. A coolness beneath my covers, in place of her body heat. Twelve, our move to the city, to Alexandria, at the beginning of the school year. That seemed weight enough for both our shoulders. I sold the piano. X had a short-lived fling with smoking cigarettes. Now, thirteen, and suddenly he is too old for all that.

It could be that I am avoiding the issue. Nine months ago, I went to the library and xeroxed copies of the male and female anatomy, those full-body biology textbook shots, intending to make my presentation to him. I wanted to keep it clinical, the way I would have shown a customer at my veterinary that their dog was having pregnancy complications. My intention was to leave love out of it. On my way home, I saw a terrifying vision of what I would do when the conversation turned to actual procedure. I pictured myself placing the male copy on top of the female copy, between my hands, and rubbing my palms together. I broke out in a humiliated sweat. I jerked the car over to the curb and slipped the pages into a gutter. X probably knows the basics already. What he doesn't know, the smooth way morning light looks on a woman's skin, the way her hair can play between bare shoulder blades, Grace across the way, with her potted daisies on the windowsill, will surely teach him.

*   *   *

To the uninitiated, it would appear that Grace Poole has re-nounced clothing altogether. She has dark curly hair, all of it, and wild eyebrows and is so pale as to be distracting. It's true that she walks from room to room naked. Sleeps and feeds her dog, watches television, and eats breakfast without clothes. Grace spends almost all of her time at home, clothesless. These things I have learned in the four days since I discovered my son's little secret. And his home-work fetish began almost two weeks ago, just about the time our new neighbor arrived.

When she does go out, Grace makes the act of getting dressed something almost unbearably alluring. The slow taking away of my guilty pleasure. She makes her body a secret again, dressing slowly, as if she regretted having to do it at all. A reverse striptease; I imagine balloons inflating around her as she pulls pins out of them. The sight of her rolling panty hose over lightly muscled calves and dimpled knees, tugging them over the crescent folds where her supple thighs meet her bottom, shifting her hips side to side, or standing in the middle of the room, slipping her arms into the sleeves of a clean shirt, buttoning it over her breasts, breaks my heart. I have not seen a naked woman since my wife was alive.

Now, Grace is talking on the telephone. She has six phones, each one a different color, lined up on a card table against her downstairs window. My first thought was phone sex, but that would be too per-fect. She is standing behind the table, arms crossed beneath her breasts, lifting her brown nipples, pinning the phone against her shoulder with her cheek. I can just make out the blue earpiece in all that hair. The wall behind her is lined with cardboard boxes, stacked three high, each one imprinted with the same logo—a rust-colored rooster—and writing in Spanish. I hear my son trotting down the stairwell and just have time to drop the shade in my study and stash the binoculars between the chair and my lower back before he opens the door. I can't get my hands on any documents to look busy, so I stare at the ceiling and pretend that I was daydreaming. Watching Grace seems like daydreaming sometimes, languorous as jasmine.

"Shouldn't you be working, Dad?" X says. "Somebody's got to put food on the table around here." He is standing just inside the room, still in his school uniform, gray slacks and blue shirt, now untucked. X is blond and tan and brown-eyed. He looks exactly like his mother. I try to find traces of myself in him when he doesn't know I'm watching. While he sleeps, his cheeks flushed with dreaming. At dinner, sitting in front of the television, holding his plate near his chin, his eyes half closing when he lifts a mouthful. Usually, I don't find anything, and when I do, those things are fleeting, an expression, a gesture, gone almost as soon as I've seen them. The sight of him, of his mother in him, makes me feel guilty about watching Grace. He is smiling strangely, and I can't tell if he is on to me.

"I thought maybe we could do something together after school," I lie. "I didn't know you'd have so much *homework.*"

I say homework in italics, hoping to catch him off guard, to put him on the defensive for a change. He leans into the door frame, shoves a hand into his pocket. I can hear the muffled thump of a tennis ball on the public courts across the street.

"Yeah, well." He shrugs and looks in the direction of the tennis sounds.

"Besides, I'm on emergency call tonight. I thought an afternoon off would do me some good." This is the truth. I have become part of an arrangement of the three local vets, where one of us stays on call twenty-four hours on alternating nights. The other offices transfer their emergency patients after business hours. "So, what do you say? Should we go down to the mall and look at that CD player you want?"

He brightens visibly.

"Cool," he says. "Let me change clothes and we're gone."

He pivots on a heel and goes stomping back upstairs.

After my wife died, I moved my son from our farm in Loudon County to this place, a brick town house in Alexandria, anonymous among the rows of similar buildings. Ours wasn't a working farm, just some land, the old farmhouse and the sagging barns behind it, and a grain silo that Sarah called the Leaning Tower of Loudon. My practice has boomed since our move to the city. My clientele, though, has changed from horses and hearty dogs to mostly cats and those dogs that need constant grooming. Poodles and such, city dogs. I never would have thought that grooming would become a vital part of my practice, but I've recently hired an assistant, Sissy, for just that purpose. Sissy is young and attractive and people like her, and the owners of my new patients seem to find something charming, something quaint, in having a country doctor for their pets. I make my manner brusque and forceful and have lately found myself speaking in colloquialisms to fit the part that has been given me. They often ask why a veterinarian, a natural lover of animals, does not have a pet of his own. I mention lack of space and the inclemency of keeping animals confined to the city. A happy dog is a running dog, I say. I made that up. And they nod and look at the floor, guilty in their minds of animal cruelty. They like my subtle scolding.

What I don't tell them is that I once saw a Siberian husky called Bear run over by a lumber truck, flatbed strapped with skinned trees. This was before X was born, and Sarah and I loved that dog as if he were our child. She would put a plate for him under the dinner table so he could have his meals with us. On cold nights, he slept in the bed between us, his head on a polyester pillow that Sarah bought because it turned out he was allergic to down. All of us slept on polyester pillows. I still do. To console her on the evening of the accident, I had to promise that we would never have another pet. I'm not certain how serious she was about the promise, whether it was just one of those things people did at a time of tragedy, self-denial as punishment for some implicit fault in the affair, but our farm was without animals until her death.

X found a cat curled up in the grain silo the month after Sarah's funeral and I gave in to his pleading and let us keep it. The cat was never fond of me, ignored my attempts at affection, hissing at my touch and rushing to X for protection. The cat wouldn't eat until the kitchen lights were off and I had gone up to bed. Late one night, I went down to the kitchen for a snack and flipped the light switch and surprised him at his bowl. He skittered across the linoleum, out of the little pet door and our lives. We never saw him again. I tried fish, after the cat, for X's sake, but could never remember to feed them or change their water and when I did remember, I thought of Sarah and the promise that I made.

Grace Poole and her shar-pei, Candle, are new patients of mine. I have never found any truth in the idea that people and their pets come to look alike over time. Candle is all wrinkles and short, wiry hair and full of high-strung motion. They have only been in once, for a flea dip and groom, but Sissy noticed something about Grace immediately. Sissy is nineteen and always teasing me about not dating. While Grace was filling out her paperwork, she pulled me aside and said, "Bingo. That's the one. Ask her out, Dr. Shaw. We'll double. You can set me up with that pretty son of yours."

She also teases X, when he sometimes comes in to earn his allowance after school. Both of us, X and I, clearly enjoy it.

"Can't. She's my new neighbor," I said. "If it didn't work out, I would always be running into her at the mailbox."

"If you don't get a date soon, the customers are going to think you're gay. Think about what that would do to business," she said.

After X left for school today, I called the office, told Sissy and my other assistant, Roy, to take the day off, and spent the morning watching Grace. From the window in my study, I can see into her kitchen and living room, but when she went to the second floor, I had to dash up to X's room and crouch on his bed, where I imagine he must watch her. Our separation on the stairwell was torturous. The dog followed her everywhere. I wondered what my son thinks when he does his spying. I crossed my arms on the sill, the way he does, and pressed my forehead to the cool glass. I pulled his blanket over my shoulders. She must seem to him unreal, a gift so lucky, so fantastic, he can hardly believe in her. I pictured him saying honest prayers that she wouldn't go away, the image so perfect and fragile that to touch her, to even imagine touching her, might make her come apart in wisps of smoke. X's return from school confined me to the study, and now I have lied my way into having to leave the house altogether, but I don't mind really.

One thing has impressed me about X since my discovery. He hasn't brought anyone over to watch with him. When I was his age, the first thing I would have done was have a dozen friends lined up at the window eating popcorn or something. Having a secret to share made me feel important. But not X. He doesn't want to share her. He doesn't want to spoil whatever it is he's feeling up there. I hope he doesn't know that he's splitting time with his father.

It is almost five o'clock by the time we leave. X is very careful when dressing for the mall. He has selected a plain white T-shirt from the Gap, Levi's jeans, and brand-new Nike high-tops. Close to two hundred dollars for the whole outfit. I had no idea. His mother did all his shopping. I have suits that cost less, and, except for the shoes, he looks like a fifties hoodlum. I half expect him to roll a pack of cigarettes in his shirtsleeve.

We drive a while, all interstate and highway on the way to the mall, and X is quiet, maybe thinking about his CD player, maybe thinking about Grace. The breeze from the open window whips his hair. I let myself think about Grace, too. I'm not sure how I will re-act when I see her again in person. In the flesh, so to speak. Our meeting, as neighbors, as doctor/patient, is inevitable. I wonder sometimes if she knows that she is being watched, if the absence of curtains on her windows is deliberate, and not, as I tell myself, just because she's new to town. I don't think she knows that her vet lives next door—the last four days, I've been getting my mail under cover of darkness—but I wonder if she can feel our eyes on her, if the two of us are giving off some kind of lonely vibe. X is staring, blank-eyed, in front of us. Our thoughts of Grace fill the car as palpably as the quick air.

"How about you roll that window up and let's get some AC go-ing," I say.

He rolls his eyes at me but does as I ask. He turns on the radio, and I turn it down a little. X does a sigh, one that is full of implications.

"Dad, I need to ask a favor," he says. "There's this girl I want to ask out, and I was wondering if you'd drive us to the movies. Her parents could drive, but they're real old, and they want to drive too much, you know. They're happy-assed about stuff like that. They get off on participating."

At first, I'm panicked. He's going to ask Grace to the movies. But that's absurd and besides, Grace has her driver's license. At the same time, I'm unreasonably happy that he's asked me to be their chauffeur. I struggle to withhold a barrage of questions. I turn the radio back up.

"Sounds like fun," I say.

He nods and grows remote again. A woman in an antique convertible, a DeSoto or something, passes us on X's side. It has fins and everything, makes her look like a movie star. Both of us turn to look.

I say, "How would you feel about your old man getting a date soon?"

"Cool," he says.

"That wouldn't bother you?" I'm surprised.

"No way," he says.

"Understand that I loved your mother. I will always love your mother," I say.

"Mom's dead," he says. "She'd understand."

X is a man of few words, the strong, silent type. Add a scuffed leather motorcycle jacket to his outfit and he could double for Marlon Brando in *The Wild One*. X's mother died of an infection resulting from her tubal ligation. Almost an unheard-of cause of death, the doctors said, but this I already knew. Even vets know a thing or two about people medicine. Sarah was alive in the hospital less than a week. I had always wanted a big family, wanted the constant clamor of children in our house, but there were medical reasons for the operation, and Sarah softened things by saying how much the idea of raising an only child appealed to her. We could spoil him rotten, give him whatever he wanted. She wouldn't have to divide her love, she said. Two ways was enough.

I have never actually admitted the possibility of dating again, though I have begun to entertain it more and more recently. Particularly with Sissy's insistence and the arrival of Grace Poole. The reawakening of those boyhood desires. Naked is, after all, still naked, even to a thirty-six-year-old widower.

The mall is massive and intimidating, but X moves through it easily, as if it were his natural habitat. He wanted me to give him the credit card and wait in the car. He told me he was a smart shopper. I told him that was quite possibly the most hysterical thing I had ever heard. He grabs my arm and jerks me along when I stop at the map to look for the stereo store. He knows where he is going and remains, always, about three paces ahead of me. In front of a store called Southern Culture, he freezes and raises his hand to me, fist clenched, like a soldier walking point. He is so definite in his motion that I go still as well. I think he must have seen that in a Vietnam movie.

"Wait here," he says.

I do as I am told. X weaves through the steady flow of shoppers, across the wide aisle, to three girls who look about his age. They are standing in front of a pet store, one of those places where the animals are caged behind a glass wall. The girls look happy to see X. He gives them all a smile and pushes his fingers through his hair, his mother's hair, weightless and golden. They laugh at something he says and one of the girls, the prettiest, lays a hand on his shoulder. X doesn't acknowledge the hand, lets her leave it there, waits for them to finish laughing. He's doing an eyebrow raise, as if surprised that they could find him so funny, so charming. My son is a natural. He would probably do better with Grace Poole than I would. X looks over his shoulder at me, casually, sees me watching, and gives me a dirty look. I spin around to face the shop window. Southern Culture specializes in reproduction antebellum antiques. Polymers where there should be pine. Porch jockeys with machine-induced paint chips.

In the window directly in front of me is an awkward-looking fake antique telephone, black with brass cradle and receivers, the works. I don't think there were telegraphs before the Civil War, much less telephones, but seeing it there makes me wonder what Grace Poole could be up to with all those phones. Her conversations only last a minute or two and she takes notes while she is talking. I never heard of a phone sex girl taking notes, except maybe to get credit card numbers, and she does too much writing for that to be the explanation.

X returns and leads me to the stereo store. He has a short discussion with the salesgirl, who is very attractive and all business. She is wearing a tan, ankle-length skirt, slit open to the knee. She is impressed with my son's knowledge of electronics and shows me the model that he wants. It holds ten CDs and is apparently the only type made on earth that can continue playing while the carriage is ejected and still rotating. On sale for $1,300, speakers and receiver not included. I ask if that's a feature he absolutely must have.

"It's the best, Dad," he says. "Think of it as a long-term investment."

X has one arm crossed at his stomach, cupping the elbow of the other arm in his palm. He is stroking his chin, one foot forward, weight back, as if regarding a masterpiece of art.

"Tell me again," I say. "Whose child are you?"

The salesgirl looks from X to the CD player and back to X.

"He'll definitely be getting his money's worth, Dad," she says.

"It is, unfortunately, and I'm sure much to both of your disappointments, not his money," I say.

We settle on something more reasonable.

In the car, X is again silent. I have embarrassed him both in front of his friends by staring and in front of the salesperson by being cheap. Six hundred dollars isn't cheap in my estimation, but clearly X is disappointed. I resent his sullenness and try to get him talking again.

"What about Grace Poole?" I say. "Our new neighbor."

He tenses a little but doesn't look at me.

"What about her?" he says.

"You know, for my date," I say. "We could double. Miss Poole and I could go to the movies with you and your girlfriend."

X turns his head slowly to look at me. He is angry. Before the last words are out of my mouth, I understand that it was the wrong thing to say, that I said it to provoke him. He gives me a mean, shallow laugh.

"She's so out of your league," he says.

Three months after Sarah died, I broke X's wrist. We were on the lawn playing football and he was running wildly by me, at the point in our game when I would let him go past me, through the pair of apple trees we used as a goal line. Let him do his touchdown dance, spike the ball, spread his arms like wings, and prance in a circle. I ran after him and caught him from behind, wrapping him up, jarring the ball loose, driving him down. His arm went out to brace himself and the wrist snapped audibly. X carried his cast, proudly, like a club.

X won't let me help him assemble his new stereo. He doesn't even allow me to help him carry it from the car. I return to the study, lock the door behind me, and take up my binoculars. Grace is on the phone, a pink one this time, and she is wearing a cream-colored bra, but that is all, like she was just getting ready to dress when the phone rang. She scratches a pencil across a pad, tears the sheet loose, and jams it down on a thin spike attached to a metal base. I can't see the dog. Grace never does get up to dress, which I am glad of, just keeps on answering the phones, first one, then another, putting one on hold and coming back to it. She is a popular lady. I can't figure out the phones.

It isn't long before my house is full of music. I go out of the study and stand at the bottom of the stairwell to let the sound come down to me more clearly. There are long windows on either side of the front door leaking weak light into the foyer. The song that X is playing sounds familiar, something from the seventies, heavy with feedback guitars, but I can't put my finger on its name. Probably, I heard it on the office radio. Sissy likes that sort of music, calls it classic.

And suddenly, I'm remembering Sarah and me, trying to manhandle a piano through the front door of our farmhouse. X was maybe seven, too small to help, so he supervised. The piano was on a dolly, but even so we kept banging it into walls and furniture, filling the house with resonant discord, and the air was full of the smell of hay grass—someone was always cutting hay out there, if not on our land then on the next farm down the road. Just follow the white wooden fence—a sweet smell, like the cakes Sarah would try to bake and botch, more often than not, leaving them in the oven too long or screwing up the recipe. Dessert was the most hilarious time of day in our house, cakes looking like deflated footballs, pies blackened like bituminous coal. It made me hungry, that smell. I was always hungry in Loudon County.

X was trying to talk his mother into letting him have a horse just before she died. He had nearly convinced her to break her promise. She was, after all, the one who wanted to spoil him. X guaranteed that he would let us choose the horse, if he was allowed to give it a name. For X, this was a major concession. I never said anything directly to him, but after he was asleep and Sarah and I were alone in bed, I would argue against this idea—not the horse itself but X choosing the name. A horse is too noble an animal. I see horses every day with ridiculous, childish names, I said. Black Beauty, Sox, Paint. I had a patient called Fanny. It's degrading to them, Sarah. She told me that if there was going to be a horse, which there probably wouldn't, it would be X's and X should name it. She would prop her back against the headboard and smoke cigarettes, tipping ashes into a ceramic bowl on her lap. Smoking was her secret vice; she didn't want X to know that his mother sanctioned such a nasty habit. What are you talking about, Byron? she'd say. You're the one that's being juvenile. I wonder now what name he would have chosen. The boy who has nicknamed himself after a letter in the alphabet.

When I take up my binoculars again, Grace is nowhere to be found. Almost a half hour passes, the light fading between our homes, without a trace of her. She must have gone up for the night.

She is X's until dawn. I would like to creep upstairs and stand in his doorway, the door just slightly open, and watch him watching her. Not to catch him red-handed but just to look at him, see if he is the same sort of voyeur as his father.

Grace comes running down the stairs into my line of sight. She stops in the middle of the room, breathless, harried, and stands there, one hand pushed up into that mass of brown hair, holding it back away from her forehead. Her lips are moving, but I can't see who she's talking to. She walks over to the black phone, picks it up and starts to dial, then stops and drops the receiver on the table and runs back upstairs. When she returns, the dog is in her arms, her back arched under its weight. Candle is not moving in a way that is frightening. Not loose and recently dead but stiff, body wracked with sporadic trembling. My first thought is Lyme disease, but that's unlikely. The disease is carried by ticks that don't exist in the city. I saw it dozens of times in the country.

Grace lays Candle on the table, using her elbow to move the phones. She finds a phone book and begins rifling through it, back, then forward again, as if she were having trouble concentrating. I realize, suddenly, that she is looking for my number. I retrieve my own phone book from the desk drawer and look for her name, but it isn't there. That makes sense, she's new to town. Besides, I couldn't call her. She would know that I had been spying on her.

I watch her stop turning pages, watch her dial and speak into the receiver, but my phone never rings. I think, at first, that she has called another vet, that she didn't like me when I met Candle the first time. I'm crushed. But, finally, my phone rings. It is Sissy. She's manning the office line tonight.

"Get your act together," she says. "We've got an emergency call. Grace Poole. Her dog is sick. Maybe tonight's your big chance, Dr. Shaw. A woman with a sick dog. She'll be super vulnerable." She waits a moment for me to laugh and, when I don't, becomes professional again. "The dog is paralyzed except for muscle spasms. She's coming in."

"I know," I say.

"What?"

"Nothing," I say. "I'll be right there."

I am holding the binoculars in one hand, the phone in the other. Grace has disappeared upstairs, momentarily, and returns carrying a bundle of clothes. I watch her dress. She pulls on walking shorts, cut high and flattering, and a T-shirt. She is barefoot and doesn't bother with underwear. Candle, she gathers in her arms, and burdened with the dog, she can't open the door. It is all I can do not to go outside, cross the little alley between us, and help her.

I wait until I hear Grace's car door close, hear the engine start. Wait until her headlights pass my window, casting shadows, before I get up to leave. I find X in the foyer, sitting at the bottom of the stairs. It is almost dark and he is brushed with the last delicate light from the street.

"I want to go," he says.

We look at each other for a long moment, neither of us speaking. X is still wearing his mall clothes. He looks worried but never takes his eyes away from mine. For an instant, I think I see something familiar in his face, something that I recognize. It is at those moments, when the veneer of his confidence has cracked just a little, when he shows, like light creeping under a doorway, in his eyes, in the set of his mouth, traces of being a boy, that I imagine a little of myself in him. It is at those moments when I love him most.

"Okay," I say.

My clinic is only a few blocks away, but the drive is intolerable. I force myself to go slowly, to brake at every stop sign, to signal at every corner. X won't look at me, keeps his eyes on other people's houses, the warmth of their lighted windows. Grace is crying by the time we reach the office, sitting Indian-style in one of the plastic waiting room chairs. There are circles of dirt on the balls of her feet, and I can see a shadow on her thigh made by the leg of her shorts. I remember that she isn't wearing underwear. When we come in, she wipes her eyes and tries to fix her hair, which is wild and spiraling. She is very beautiful like that. X is wide-eyed. I think he is amazed to be seeing her in person, amazed that she exists beyond those windows.

I can't think of a suitable colloquialism, so I say, "It's going to be all right, Miss Poole."

Sissy and the dog are in the examination room waiting for me. Candle is still trembling, her I.D. tag clinking against the examination table's metal surface.

"Her temperature is high," Sissy says. "That's all I knew to do until you got here."

"Lyme disease," I say.

I look around the door to the waiting room. X is sitting about four chairs over from Grace, looking petrified, eyes glued to the floor.

"Miss Poole, has this dog been out of the city recently? Camping or something?" I say.

"Yes," she says. "About a week ago."

"Any ticks on her?"

"A few," she says. She is calming some.

"Good," I say. "I'll get her fixed up."

I wish I could stop talking like a country doctor, just for a minute. I push my fingers through Candle's fur until I find what I'm looking for, the bull's eye reddening of a tick bite at her shoulder. I give the dog a muscle relaxant to stop the spasms and a shot of tetracycline for the Lyme's, because it won't hurt her either way. I have Sissy take a blood sample. These are the things I understand. This is the place where I know what I am doing. I stroke the dog, pulling all that loose skin out straight, then letting it wrinkle up again, until she quiets. I whisper nonsense in her ear. Pretty dog, pretty dog. Tell your mother good things about Dr. Shaw.

"That dog was messed up," Sissy says. "It's a good thing you were home and not out painting the town like you usually are."

"Hoot with the owls at midnight, and you can't fly with the eagles at dawn," I say. I smile at her.

"C'mon, Dr. Shaw," she says, rolling her eyes in the direction of the waiting room.

X and Grace are talking when I go back into the other room. They don't hear me come in. X is smiling, but differently from the mall, nervous and grateful for her attention. He is tapping his feet, wringing his hands. Grace seems relaxed, settled some. It hasn't occurred to me until now to wonder how old she is. Maybe twenty-eight, twenty-nine, not too young. Somewhere between X and me but closer to me. There are a lot of things I hadn't thought to wonder about her.

"Candle is going to be good as new," I say.

They look up at me, lips parted slightly, surprised to find me there.

"That's great," X says. His enthusiasm is genuine.

"Thank you so much, Dr. Shaw," she says, standing, taking a few steps in my direction. "Sorry I got so emotional there. That isn't like me. It's Candle. Do you have pets?"

"I have X," I say. "He's sort of like a pet."

She smiles and looks back at my son, who, to my surprise, is also smiling. X is watching me, not angry, but definitely watching, waiting to see what I will do.

"A very cute and charming pet he is," she says. "Does he do any tricks? Sit, X. Roll over, boy."

"Grace is in the mail order business, Dad," he says, too eagerly. "She does clothes for this Venezuelan company. Environmentally correct sweaters and stuff."

X and Grace. They are on a first-name basis. She waves his comment away and says, "I just got the job. They're a penny-ante operation. Won't even give me a computer or an office phone. I have to do everything by hand."

"Really?" I say.

My heart starts kicking, my tongue goes gummy in my mouth. At least that explains the phones. Now, I know something else about her. What I don't know is what to talk to her about. I can't very well talk about the fact that I've been spying on her. I can't tell her that I see her in my sleep. I launch headlong into my spiel about Lyme disease—It's an inflammatory disease, I say, caused by tick-borne spirochete. The symptoms include joint pains, fatigue, and sometimes neurological disturbances. I hear my voice, droning on like a nightmare biology teacher, but I can't shut up. Did you know that this disease was named for Lyme, Connecticut, where a particularly deadly outbreak was studied? She nods along with my words, trying to seem interested. I force myself to stop talking. I remember X and how at ease he was with those girls at the mall. I run my fingers through my hair, smile the smile, and cock my hip like some kid. It doesn't feel right, feels foolish. The proper words for this moment— Grace in the washed-out light from the fluorescent bulbs, X with his hands in his pockets, his eyes full of sympathy—do not exist. I am aware that nothing can happen between us, not after what X and I have been doing the last few days, but I don't want it to be over just yet. Any moment now, I think, and she will disappear.

Dogfight

Hi John sent both Bill Hoffman and his Great Dane to the hospital. Being an Irish setter, Hi John was generally a gentle dog and got along fine with the other neighborhood pets and, Reed knew, even once had a romantic thing going with Mrs. Bishop's springer spaniel across the street. Reed and Hi John were jogging at night, and the sky was full of distracting white stars, and maybe that's why Reed didn't see the Great Dane from two houses down, the Hoffmans' house, come tearing into the street, toenails clicking on the pavement. Hi John's first instinct was to run for home, to go in the opposite direction of the oncoming Dane, but Reed wasn't quick enough. His own first instinct was to go completely still and hope that the danger passed. He didn't think of running, though he was only maybe thirty yards from his front door, until he felt Hi John tugging the leash in terror. And that was far too late.

The Great Dane, huge and white with a black head, was on Hi John, clamping down on his neck, his lips pulled back in an angry rictus. The darkness made things more frightening. Everything slow and jerky like watching an old silent movie, each frame distinguishable. He saw glimpses—bared teeth, fur damp with what might have been blood, maybe just saliva, twists of angry motion—all underscored with growls and whines of pain. Bill Hoffman and his wife,

April, didn't come out of their yard, just stayed on the damp grass, calling their dog.

Reed had been told never to interfere in a dogfight, but he couldn't bring himself to let go of the leash. He felt that if he let go, Hi John would be killed. He began beating the Dane with his fists and whipping it with the end of the leash. Reed was afraid to tears for Hi John. At that moment, he believed that he could not go on living if anything happened to his dog.

"Goddamnit," he shouted to Hoffman, "get out here and grab your fucking dog. Right now."

Bill Hoffman edged nervously into the street, circling the fight, his wife pushing him forward, Reed being pulled around helplessly, still shouting at Hoffman, cursing at him. He threatened to burn their house down while Hoffman and his wife slept, if anything happened to Hi John. Hoffman got behind his dog and grabbed him, one hand on his collar, one around his throat, and the dogs for a brief instant came apart. What surprised Reed most was that Hi John didn't take the opportunity to retreat. Instead, he lunged for the Dane's neck, so suddenly that Reed couldn't stop him, and bit Hoffman's hand by mistake. Reed could hear the bone coming apart. Hoffman pulled his injured hand away, his whole body recoiling, and at the same time, he lifted the Dane by the collar with the other hand, forepaws off the ground, belly exposed. Hi John, that quick, bit the other dog on the balls and the Dane made a sound of true pain, a howl like nothing Reed had ever heard.

Hi John kept them moving back toward their yard with a volley of barks and growls, and strained at the leash to get back into the fight. April Hoffman walked down the street to them. She was wearing a knee-length blue nightgown, made sheer and lovely by the glow of the street lamps, and her hair was down and her legs were nice. Reed was feeling strong and dizzy with adrenaline. She knelt by Hi John, who was himself again, pushing against her legs, letting her stroke his back. Her husband was screaming that they had to go to the hospital and Reed wasn't sure if he meant for himself or for his dog.

"You're a brave dog," she said to Hi John. "You wouldn't start a fight, would you? It's just that awful dog of Bill's."

She looked up at Reed. He was panting and could not stop himself from smiling. He saw everything, the moon, the pale sheen of night clouds, branches silhouetted against light from windows. This woman with a smooth face and slight widow's peak. Her husband was still calling her, getting angry, crying now. She stood slowly and looked once more at Reed before walking home.

His ex-wife, Maggie, was in his living room when he came in. She lived in the house directly behind his, separated from him only by a fence, and still had her key. In this neighborhood, though, Reed rarely locked his doors. They had been divorced for just over a year. Maggie was short and thin and it had been said by their friends that Reed and Maggie looked startlingly alike. Both blue-eyed, with the same wiry brown hair, both with identically sharp features, both small. They had more than once, in the four years they were married, been mistaken for brother and sister. The fact of their resemblance came to bother Reed after a while. He believed it to be unusual and quite possibly unhealthy and once, coming face to face with her in a dark hallway, still drowsy from sleeping, he had thought he was seeing himself, having some sort of out-of-body experience. Reed was so shaken up that he slept on the couch for two nights and never explained to Maggie.

"I heard all the commotion," Maggie said. "Is Hi John okay?"

They sat on the floor, one on either side of Hi John, and searched for wounds. A few scratches, one cut behind his ear that was particularly nasty, that Reed promised he would have looked at on the way to work in the morning. Hi John beat the floor with his tail and tried to roll over so they could scratch his stomach.

"You should have seen him," Reed said. "We kicked ass, didn't we, boy?"

"Don't make him think that fighting is good," Maggie said, irritated. "He could have been hurt."

"Maggie's right, Hi John. Don't fight. But if you have to fight, show no mercy. Go for the balls. Maximum violence with all available speed." He patted Hi John's stomach and scratched him until his leg began working the air.

Reed told Maggie about the fight, in detail, about beating the other dog with his fists and about thinking that Hi John was going to be killed. He paced the rug. When he got to the part about Hi John biting Bill Hoffman and then the Dane's testicles, imitating the sound the Dane made and doing a souped-up parody of Hoffman crying for his wife like a little boy, Maggie started laughing. She rocked back on the floor, hair spreading out beneath her and stomped her feet. He was excited from the telling and threw himself down next to her and tried to kiss her. She pushed him away, still laughing, and said, "Serves the bastard right." There had been, shortly after the divorce and Maggie's move around the corner, a questionable omission from the guest list of a neighborhood party.

They watched television until the blue lights of a police siren splashed against the window. Maggie had fallen asleep with her head in his lap. They walked out together and stood embarrassed while the other neighbors came out onto their lawns to see the commotion, to see who had brought the police, lights flashing threats, into this part of town. Joan Bishop lived directly across the street and was standing alone on her porch, haloed by the light coming from the open door behind her. She was an older woman, white-haired, long-ago widowed. When Reed waved, she stepped back into the house, quickly, and shut the door. He could see a curtain ease back, the shape of her face at the window.

The policewoman, who was thick and black and quite possibly the largest woman Reed had ever seen, explained that this was only routine, that any time someone came into the emergency room with a dog bite, it had to be looked into.

"Are they pressing charges?" Maggie asked. "What sort of charges do you press in a case like this? Their dog started the fight."

The policewoman became confused when Maggie explained that,

yes, she was one of the dog's owners, along with Reed, but that, no, she didn't actually see the fight or even actually live with Reed anymore but that, yes, she lived in the house directly behind his and, yes, she had said they were divorced. She told too much. She said that they were no longer married but that they still cared for one another and that neither of them wanted to part with the dog. There were irreconcilable differences that they could not live with married but that they could accept divorced, as neighbors. Reed watched and listened, quietly, thankful that she didn't go into the differences. He was thinking that sometimes Maggie could be quite pretty and that this was one of those times. He liked the way her hands moved when she spoke.

"The law is that your dog has to be quarantined ten days for rabies observation," the officer said when Maggie finished. "Could I see the animal?"

Reed went inside and brought Hi John out on his leash. When Hi John saw this woman and the colored lights and all the neighbors watching, he tensed and began barking savagely. Reed tried to settle him down, tried to get ahold of his collar to show his tags and that he was up to date on his shots but Hi John wouldn't be still.

"No matter," the woman said. "Shots or no shots the dog has to be quarantined. Someone will be by in the morning to get him."

They watched her drive off, Hi John barking until the car was out of sight and the neighbors had gone back inside. Reed noticed that the Hoffmans' car was still not in the driveway. Hi John settled down and everything got real quiet.

"Nice timing," Maggie said to the dog.

Reed woke bleary-eyed and confused, to a knock at the door. It was two men from the city come to take Hi John to quarantine. Reed met them at the porch in his bathrobe and offered them coffee, still too close to sleep to understand that this was the enemy. The men, deadly serious about their errand, refused. Reed went inside to collect the dog and found his solidarity there, as well. Back on the porch, Reed said, "This is a travesty. If anything, you should be locking up the Hoffmans' dog."

Hi John slapped their legs with his tail, happily.

One of the men looped a wire, attached to a long pole, around Hi John's neck and began to lead him to the van. They kept their distance, skirting Hi John carefully, like bullfighters. Reed ran out into the yard. The grass was damp and newly cut and stuck to his feet. He knelt beside Hi John and hugged his neck.

"Do your time like a man, Hi John," he said. "Don't take any shit off anybody. I'll be by to visit this afternoon."

April Hoffman came by as Reed was knotting his tie for work. She looked tired and worried and was holding a plastic baggie full of bones. The house had seemed to Reed, before her appearance, terribly quiet without Hi John, though he couldn't recall specific sounds that Hi John made when he was there. Just that energy, the electric presence of another life. She sat on the couch and Reed brought her a cup of coffee. Through the windows behind her he could see Maggie's backyard. It had begun to rain, lightly, and Maggie's careful rows of vegetables, purple eggplant, red and green peppers, fragile tomatoes, looked wilted and burdened in the drizzle.

"This is the kind of rain you hear called beautiful," she said.

"Is it?" Reed said. He wasn't at all certain how he should treat her. He didn't know whether to be angry or apologetic.

"I brought these for Hi John." She shook the bag, smiling. "Bill saves the T-bones. He would kill me if he knew I was here. I feel awful about last night. Joan Bishop told me that the police came for Hi John."

Joan Bishop had once complained that Hi John was making overtures toward her springer spaniel and that while he was making overtures—those were her exact words—he was lifting his leg on her rosebushes. Maggie wanted to know what was wrong with Hi John, why he wasn't good enough for Mrs. Bishop's dog. She said the peeing was just a manifestation of canine courtship, though Reed wasn't sure about that. Maggie called Mrs. Bishop's dog a whore. She made a case for free will. She said, just because you don't approve of our living arrangement doesn't mean you have to take it out on our dog. Reed had watched the two women arguing in the street, heard the unnatural anger rising in their voices, and he couldn't help feeling sad for Hi John. That moment was probably the end of his romance and he would never understand why. Reed knew about endings and the loss of love. Joan Bishop had avoided them since.

"He'll be incarcerated for ten days," Reed said. "How is Bill? His hand okay?"

"His hand is disgusting," April said. "He had to get a cast and his fingers are all swollen like sausages."

Reed was thinking that in all the time they had lived near the Hoffmans, maybe two years, he had never been alone with this woman. He couldn't recall ever actually speaking to her but he was sure that he must have, being neighbors. And here she was now on his couch, in a white blouse open at the neck and skirt dotted with sailboats, and sandals with straps, thin as paper, speaking as if they had known each other all their lives. He was strangely excited by her presence. He sat on the couch next to her and she crossed her legs so that her foot was just touching his shin. She looked at him over the rim of her cup.

"I'm really sorry about all this," he said. "It isn't your fault, really."

"If not for you," April said, "everything could have been a lot worse. Bill's hand will get better. Hi John could have been killed."

"I don't know," Reed said. "He was holding his own."

The phone rang and Reed walked into the kitchen to answer it. It was Maggie. Reed was nervous and excited both. He felt like he was up to something and it felt good. He pressed his fingers against the windowpane, which was cool and clammy.

"Have they come for Hi John yet?" she said.

"This morning," he said. "I can't talk right now. April Hoffman is here apologizing. She brought some bones for Hi John."

"Make sure she doesn't sue," Maggie said, before hanging up.

April was looking out the window, past beads of rainwater, toward the backyard and Maggie's house. Reed wondered if she knew what she was looking at. Her hair was swept back into a chignon and she had pulled her knees up beneath her, covering her legs with her skirt, which was cotton and loose. Her toes were peeking out from beneath it, her toenails painted creamy red. He thought he had once heard Maggie call that color coral. He wanted to ask about her marriage but thought that was a bad idea, since it would possibly raise questions about his own marriage or lack thereof and that was not something he felt comfortable talking about.

Instead he said, "This was very nice of you to come by. We don't really know each other very well, do we? That's too bad. Since we're neighbors and all."

She smiled and narrowed her eyes at him and picked up her coffee cup with both hands. She wasn't exactly what he thought of as beautiful, her face a bit too long, her eyes set too far apart, but he found himself terribly excited by her. He couldn't stop picturing bedroom scenes with her. The two of them winding together, the covers knotted at the foot of the bed. April Hoffman on her back with his fingers in her mouth. He remembered, suddenly, the commandment about coveting thy neighbor's wife. He almost laughed and knew that his smile must have been crazy and obvious. The Bible didn't acknowledge that wives could also covet. In real life, he thought, women do all the seducing. They know what they want and no amount of drinks bought or lies told can change that fact. The best you can wish for is to be the person that they want you to be in that first hopeful moment.

"Come sit by me," April said.

The primary problem in Reed's marriage to Maggie had been his own eventual impotence in her presence. The first few years had been marked by a slow tapering off of desire but this hadn't really bothered Reed. He believed it to be commonplace and attributed it, partly, to the fact of their physical resemblance. They were comfortable and they were friends. It was when Maggie slept with her secretary, a young woman whom Reed never found attractive, that his ability to perform with her stopped altogether. Maggie called it her fifteen-minute flirtation with lesbianism. Reed didn't know what to call it. One of the worst things about her sleeping with a woman was that there had been no one to lash out at, no one to hit. The event had fueled his fantasy life for months but despite the fantasies, he could not actually bring himself up to the task of sleeping with Maggie.

Reed was too thrilled to go straight to work so he drove around the block and let himself in Maggie's front door. He called to her and she said she was in the tub and he went back and sat on the toilet across from her. When she saw the look on his face, she said, "Get the cigarettes."

Neither of them smoked but when they had been married, it had been their habit to keep a pack of cigarettes around for heart-to-heart talks. Reed found them in the refrigerator in the place set aside for storing butter. They smelled musty and antique, relics from their life together. It had taken almost a year to smoke the pack half empty and would probably take another year to finish it.

He lit a cigarette for Maggie and placed it between her lips while she dried her hands. Both of them took a few shallow drags, warming to the conversation, Reed now sitting on the cold tile, leaning his back against the tub. He turned and flicked his ash into the water. Maggie dropped hers on the soap dish and waited for Reed to begin what he had come to tell her.

"I had sex with April Hoffman," he said, finally, trying to be matter-of-fact.

"You were able to sleep with her?" Maggie said.

Reed ignored this remark, let it hang in the air like the white wisps of smoke on their breath. He felt good. Maggie lifted one leg from the water and ran a washcloth over it, past her knee, along her calf.

"Where?" she said.

Reed took the washcloth from her and helped her wash her foot and ankle. When he was finished Maggie brought the other leg up and he washed it, too, stopping to dip the cloth back in the water and ring it out. He flipped his tie over his shoulder to keep it dry.

"On the floor of the living room," he said. He was holding the cigarette in his mouth to wash her leg and his voice was funny. "And in the bedroom."

"Twice?" she said. "Wow."

"No, just the one time. The floor was uncomfortable so I carried her back to the bed," he said.

Her foot was slick with soap and slipped from his hands, splashing him, spotting his blue oxford with water. He was holding his wet hands away from his body and squinting from the smoke in his eyes.

"Damn," he said.

"Sorry," she said, smiling. "Run the blow-dryer over that. Clear it right up."

He took a long drag from his cigarette and jetted the smoke in her direction. She flicked the water off her fingertips at him. Beneath the water her body looked wavy and nondescript. Reed stood and plugged in the blow-dryer near the sink and began making savage passes with it over his shirt. He was looking at her in the mirror.

"I guess, now, they won't sue us for medical bills," Maggie said.

"What?" Reed couldn't hear her over the blow-dryer.

"I guess now they won't sue."

"On the contrary," Reed shouted. "I think a suit is more inevitable now than ever. I did, after all, sleep with the man's wife."

He laughed and looked at his own reflection, then back at hers over his shoulder. He couldn't see her face, because of where the tub was situated, just her knees, rising like little islands from the water. He saw her hand appear briefly, drop an ash into the water between her knees and disappear again. His shirt was drying nicely.

"I wish you wouldn't sleep with her again," Maggie said.

"What?" Reed said, not hearing clearly.

"Never mind," she said.

"What?"

Maggie leaned over the edge of the tub to look at him. In the mirror, he could see her face, flushed from being in the water so long, the damp ends of her hair, her breasts pushed against the wall of the tub. Never mind, she said, again, but still he couldn't hear her. He could see her lips moving but couldn't understand what she was trying to say.

After some threatening glances and a surreptitious twenty palmed across the counter, the attendant at the pound agreed to let Reed take Hi John outside for a little while. There was a yard in the back where they took the dogs to do their business. Hi John was being kept in a small cage that they used for solitary confinement, hard cases only. He swaggered past the other dogs in the community cage, a different sort of criminal, and they watched him pass, enviously, a little afraid, the way Reed imagined petty thieves goggled at mob assassins.

Reed left his job at the Historical Preservation Society an hour early every day for his visits. Maggie took the afternoons, Reed the evenings. And the two of them, Reed and Hi John, sat at the fence, looking out, watching the streams of passing cars, Hi John's head turning slowly to follow each one. Reed brought the bones that April Hoffman had left and told his dog about their affair. About April coming over the last three mornings after her husband was gone. Telling him every detail, the way April breathed, deep and slow even at their most excited, the way her hair kept getting stuck to his lips. He liked that he could smell her on his clothes long after she was gone. The telling pleased him as much as the act itself. He asked about Maggie's visits, too, but Hi John didn't have anything to say, just listened without comment, cracking the bones with his teeth, the sound like branches snapping off in winter air.

"What do you two talk about out there?" the attendant said, mockingly, as Reed was on his way out.

"Women," Reed said.

They looked at each other, not speaking. The man opened his mouth, as if to say something, then snapped it shut and went back to the paperwork on his desk. Reed was surprised to find himself disappointed. Outside, the sun was shocking. It was as bright, Reed thought, as he had ever seen it.

A strange thing happened between Reed and Maggie when they got married. They had been living together for a year already and neither of them believed that a ceremony in a church for the sake of their parents would affect their relationship one way or another. Life would be business as usual, Maggie working for the county prosecutor's office, Reed overseeing the affairs of local Civil War battlefields for the Preservation Society. After dark, they would come home at roughly the same time, alternate nights cooking dinner, watch Letterman on the couch, make the kind of genial love they had grown used to, filled still with desire but regular and pretty and easy. Something did happen, though neither of them ever mentioned it, and it had nothing to do with the arm of the law or the eyes of God. It was as if a web, a delicate filigree, had been drawn between them and over the things that were theirs. This thing extended, lightly, over their past together and into the future, giving them shape, the way a sheet is thrown over the invisible man in movies to make him visible. Both of them felt it, though they might have described it differently, comforting and terrifying at the same time.

Maggie didn't want to talk about Reed's affair anymore, though he desperately wanted to tell her about it. He had to content himself with Hi John's quiet listening. She still came over at night or he went to her house and they talked of other things. The presentation that Reed was to make tomorrow to potential benefactors for Shiloh battlefield. The case Maggie was trying. But mostly they talked about Hi John.

"I don't think they're treating him well enough, do you?" Maggie said. "He looks like he's lost weight."

"Maybe he's gone on a hunger strike," Reed said.

"Don't joke," she said. "I'm serious."

"I love it when you're serious," he said.

"Look out," she said. "Somebody's being clever. Hit the dirt."

Maggie punched his arm playfully and he pretended that it hurt. He tickled her ribs and they rolled off the couch in her attempts to escape his fingers. Maggie pulled his hair and bit his shoulders and ears but not too hard and he kept on tickling her until she was in tears. The two of them rolled around this way, bunching the rug beneath them, until Maggie's leg, in a spasm of laughter, shot out and kicked a glass off the coffee table. It shattered, sprinkling the floor with shards, and brought them to their senses.

"Look what you made me do," she said. "Idiot."

Reed said, "You started it. Moron."

"Imbecile," she said.

"Ignoramus."

"Half-wit."

Later, Maggie fell asleep, leaning back against Reed on the couch with her head on his shoulder, her face turned slightly inward toward his. The television was on but he watched only her for a long time. In the dark, he could see the colors thrown off by the TV, mostly blues and reds, reflected on her skin. He could feel her breath on his neck and beneath his chin. He wanted to kiss her but he didn't, just leaned forward gently, awkwardly, so that their cheeks were together, the corners of their lips just slightly touching.

April Hoffman called in the morning to tell him that she wouldn't be stopping by today. She said it just like that. I won't be stopping by today. Reed played the moment over in his head, then went further back, like rewinding a tape, searching his memory for something he might have done wrong, something he might have said. He couldn't remember anything. Reed wasn't certain how he was supposed to feel. He knew he was supposed to feel something. At the time, he was sitting on a high stool in the kitchen, his feet hooked into its rungs, the phone on the wall near him. He felt along his arms, first one then the other, squeezing gently with his fingers, pressing against the bones, as if checking for fractures. At the elbow of the second arm, he stopped, satisfied, and let his mind wander to the coming evening. He smiled, thinking of telling Maggie that his affair was over and wondering how she would react to the news.

On his way to work, Reed ran into Joan Bishop. She was standing at the curb, rifling through the morning's mail, her hair tied down with a crimson scarf. The spaniel was with her and trotted a circle around the car. He idled behind her and rolled down the passenger window.

"Good morning, Joan," he said, leaning across the seat, smiling.

She glanced at him over her shoulder and scowled. This time of year her roses were in full bloom, practically glowing on her lawn, open to the morning, each bush surrounded by a small chicken wire fence to keep the dogs away.

"Is there something wrong?" Reed said when she didn't answer.

"Don't talk to me," she said, tucking the envelopes into her purse. She stalked away, up the gently sloping driveway toward her house, swinging her arms angrily. The dog padded along in her wake.

"Mrs. Bishop, wait," Reed said, putting the car in park and getting out. "Why don't you like me? What have I ever done to you? Is this about Hi John and your rosebushes? Is this about the dogs?"

"I don't want to talk to you," she said without looking back.

Reed had been disconcerted by this meeting and believed it was the reason his presentation wasn't going as well as he had hoped. He began at Shiloh with a bad imitation of A. S. Johnston saying to his officers, "Gentlemen, tonight we water our horses in the Tennessee." It was a nice beginning, he thought, accenting both the foolish optimism of the Confederates and the poignancy of Johnston's death in the battle. He drove the man and woman who had come this morning over the field in a golf cart, trying to conjure for them images that would be moving enough to inspire donation. The abandoned campfires, left by Union troops in the face of a surprise attack, coffeepots still warm. The small watering hole where wounded of both sides crawled for a drink, reddening the muddy water with their blood. He showed them the place where Johnston's officers cradled his head in death. The patch of ground where Beauregard's tent stood, in which he wrote to Jefferson Davis, "Grant is beaten. Will mop him up in the morning." Monuments marked each site and Reed paused a moment after he was finished to let them read. He thought if he could just get the telling right, and he told these same sad stories all the time, then they would understand the need for preservation.

"Don't you think all this glorifies the South's participation in the war?" the man said. "We have quite a few black employees and I don't know how happy it would make them to give money to something like this. The South was, after all, fighting to perpetuate slavery."

"What we are trying to glorify here, sir, is bravery," Reed said, "on both sides. We want people to come out here and be reminded of how horrible the war was. But also, to recognize the character of the participants. We can learn quite a bit from the past."

The man nodded but Reed could tell he was still unconvinced. The cart whined up a hill toward a Union graveyard, showing through a knot of trees, and the family there, taking pictures, their little boy holding a souvenir Confederate flag.

The woman said, "This isn't what I expected. I'm having a hard time seeing the big picture. I think I was expecting a football field or something."

Reed said, "That's my point. The whole thing has been trivialized by time. We need to get people out here. To sort of run the history through their fingers, if you get my meaning."

"I think someone is calling you," the man said, pointing.

Reed stopped the cart and all of them turned to look. They were parked on a cobbled path that divided a manicured lawn. To their right were rows of dilapidated cannon along a split rail fence and past those, a peach orchard, where pink and white petals blanketed the grass, pulled loose by their own creamy, lustrous weight. In the other direction, they could see a figure running through the trees, spindly white oaks, waving one arm wildly and shouting Reed's name. He must have cut over from the parking lot. They waited to let him catch up and as he got closer, Reed recognized Bill Hoffman.

"We're being charged," the woman said.

"Shit," Reed said.

"Excuse me?" the man said.

Bill Hoffman reached them, gasping, and stood a moment, hands on his knees, trying to catch his breath. He was wearing a suit and tie and his cast jutted out from beneath his sleeve. His fingers were mottled blue.

"What are you doing here, Bill?" Reed said, stepping from the cart.

"Christ," Hoffman said. "Wait a minute. I haven't run that far since high school."

"Bill?" Reed said.

"What?" Hoffman said. "What, goddamnit?"

He glanced up at Reed and their eyes met, just briefly, just long enough for Reed to notice that Hoffman's eyes were startlingly blue. Pool water blue. April must have told him everything. He doesn't know what else to do, Reed thought. He knew that feeling, desperate and weak and helpless with loss. They cut the look short at the exact same moment and both of them blushed, faces going hot, each of them having seen something private in the other's eyes.

"You don't have to go through with this," Reed said.

"You slept with my wife," Hoffman said, still breathing hard. Then to the others, pointing with his cast, "This man slept with my wife."

They were absolutely still, frozen like awkward bronze monuments.

"Look, Bill, I'm not going to do this. I won't fight you," Reed said.

Right then, Hoffman straightened and hit Reed in the temple with his cast. From the ground, Reed could see Hoffman, doubled over in pain, clutching his injured arm to his chest and he could see the sky behind him, pale, brushed occasionally with clouds. He had been about to say, it was an accident, we hadn't planned anything, it meant nothing, though all of those things, he knew, were just things you said at a time like that, even if they were true. He had been about to say, I know how you feel, I'm sorry. He didn't hurt as much as he would have expected, was just sort of dreamy and light. The man was waving his arms, the woman shouting wildly for help. Reed got to his feet, shakily, not knowing what else to do, and kicked Bill Hoffman in the groin. In the process, he lost his balance and fell on top of Hoffman and they began beating each other as best they could in such close quarters, Hoffman with his cast, pulling Reed's hair with his good hand. Reed held Hoffman in tight so he couldn't use the cast effectively and butted with his head, used his knees and elbows. They fought halfheartedly, dutifully, almost sadly, doing no less damage to each other for their lack of passion, rolling down a subtle incline, picking up fallen leaves and twigs in their hair and on their clothes, until they fell apart exhausted. The two of them lay on the grass, side by side, Hoffman's arm, the one with the cast, draped across Reed's chest, rising and falling to the rhythm of his breathing. Reed wanted to ask Hoffman if, now that he knew, he was still in love with his wife, but he didn't say anything. After a few minutes, Bill Hoffman pushed himself up and left without another word.

Reed drove to Maggie's house and let himself in the back door with the key she kept beneath an empty red clay flowerpot. He lay down on the couch in the living room and waited for her to come home. With his eyes closed, he took stock of his injuries. He must have somehow bitten his tongue, because it was swollen and felt heavy in his mouth, and by pressing it against the insides of his cheeks, he discovered a loose tooth. His face burned, as if someone had held him by the hair and dragged it back and forth across thick carpet. There was a throbbing, slow and even and only a little painful, in his temple. He could picture the bruise, a vivid discoloration, spreading back into his hairline, like a tattoo. Reed hadn't minded the horrified stares that strangers in other cars had given him on his way home. He believed, as surely as he had ever believed anything, that he deserved them. He thought of Joan Bishop, living alone in that house since her husband died. Of the morning she had called him and Maggie into her yard to tell them what Hi John had done. The roses drooping heavily on their stems that day, the petals browning at the edges. They're so fragile, she had said, they can't bear even the slightest mistreatment. He had seen Joan Bishop in the rain, another time, tying trash bags over the little wire cages to keep the flowers from being drowned.

Maggie came in slowly, wary at having found her door unlocked, and dropped her keys when she saw Reed lying in the evening shadows on her couch. He smiled crookedly at her surprise, his lips cracked and tight with dried blood.

"Oh my God," she said. "What happened to you? Were you in an accident?"

She crossed the room to him and pushed back his hair to examine his bruise. Reed moved her hands away. She was left poised, her hands inches from him, fingers curved to the shape of his head.

"Bill Hoffman and I got into a fight," he said.

"What?" she said. "That's insane. You're grown men."

"That doesn't make it any less the truth," he said.

"Let me guess," she said, holding his chin, despite his efforts to prevent her, and turning his face slowly back and forth, examining him. "Bill won. It serves you right. You look like you were thrown from a moving car."

Maggie put two fingers inside a rip in his shirt that he hadn't noticed before and touched his chest. Her fingers were cold and she left them there until they warmed a little on his skin. She plucked a bit of leaf from his hair. He turned on a lamp beside them and they squinted at each other in the new light. She was kneeling next to the couch, rocked back on her heels. He liked the way she was looking at him. Maggie stood and kicked off her shoes and padded into the kitchen.

"If he won," Reed said to the swinging door, "it was a Pyrrhic victory."

He could hear the sink running, drawers opening and closing.

"Hi John gets out tomorrow," he said. "I've been sitting here thinking we might go together to pick him up. He would like that."

"That sounds nice," she said over the rush of running water.

Maggie returned with two washcloths, one wrapping ice and another soaked in warm water. She made him slide over and sat on the edge of the couch next to him. She pressed the ice to his temple and lifted his hand to it, so he would hold it there. With the other cloth, she brushed his face, wiping his forehead first and working gently down along the bridge of his nose. The washcloth stung where it touched his wounds but in a strangely pleasant way, the way muscles ache after a long, satisfying exercise.

"I want you to tell me everything," Maggie said.

He didn't say anything for a long time, just lay still and let her press the washcloth to his cheeks, run it over his lips. She was turned to him in such a way that one side of her face was lit completely by the lamplight, the other side drawn in shadow. She pushed his eyelids gently closed with her fingertips. Water streamed down his cheeks and he thought it must have looked like he was crying.

Gerald's Monkey

Gerald wanted a monkey and Wishbone said he could get it for him. Wishbone had a man on the inside. The three of us were burning out badly rusted floor sections of a tuna rig called *Kaga* and welding new pieces in their place, patchwork repairs, like making a quilt of metal. A lot of Japanese fisheries were having ships built in the states; labor was cheaper or something. This hold was essentially a mass grave for marine life and it stunk like the dead. The smell never comes out, Gerald told me, even if you sandblasted the paint off the walls. The door to the next room had been sealed, so there was only one way in, an eight-by-ten-foot square in the ceiling, and it was almost too hot to draw breath. They seemed connected somehow, the heat and that awful smell, two parts of the same swampy thing.

"Will it be a spider monkey?" Gerald said.

Wishbone shut down his burner and looked at Gerald.

"I don't know. My Jap gets all the good shit. It'll eat bananas," Wishbone said. "It'll scratch its ass. Shit, Gerald. *Will it be a spider monkey?*"

"Spider monkeys make the best pets," Gerald said.

"Gerald, what the hell do you want with a monkey?" I said.

Gerald started to answer, paused in his burning, white sparks settling around his gloved hands, but Wishbone cut him off. He said to me, "Do not speak until you are spoken to, little man." His voice was muffled and deepened by his welding mask. "A monkey Gerald wants, a monkey Gerald gets. Now, run and fetch me some cigarettes."

He stood and stretched his legs. Wishbone was one large black man. With his welding mask down and black leather smock and gloves and long, thick legs running down into steel-toed work boots, he looked like a badass Darth Vader.

"Wishbone, can you read?" I said.

He snapped his mask up. His face was running with sweat and his eyes were bloodshot and angry. He was high on something. This was my second summer at my uncle's shipyard, and the best I could tell, Wishbone was always high.

"Did you speak, little man? I hope not."

I didn't say anything else, just pointed at the sign behind him— DO NOT SMOKE, painted in red block letters on plywood. The torches burn on a combination of pure oxygen and acetylene and sometimes tiny holes wear in the lines from use. The welding flames themselves generally burn off all the leaking oxygen and gas, but shut down the torches and give the gas a little time to collect in the air, then add a spark, and the world is made of fire. A spark is rarely enough but why test the percentages? There's a story around the yard about a guy who'd been breathing the fumes for hours with his torch unlit. When he went to fire it up, he inhaled a spark and the air in his lungs ignited. Afterward, he looked okay on the surface, nothing damaged, but his insides were charcoal, hollowed out by fire.

Wishbone glanced over his shoulder at the sign, looked back at me, shrugged. He reached under his smock and came out with a rumpled pack of Winstons. He put a bent cigarette between his lips, struck a match, and held it just away from the tip.

"This is my last cigarette," he said. "You have till I am finished to get your ass up from the floor and out to the wagon for a new pack. Let me be clear. If you are not back before I put my boot on this thing, I'm gonna beat you like a rented mule." He spoke real slow like I was his Jap connection and my English wasn't so good. "Do you understand?"

I got to my feet reluctantly. I didn't want him to know that I was afraid. I said, "Gerald, you need anything?" Gerald shook his head and gave me a wave.

I sidled to the ladder and climbed it slow and easy, no hurry, but once topside, I was gone, the fastest white boy on earth, dumping equipment as I ran, a jackrabbit, skirting welders and shipfitters on the deck, clanging down the gangplank, then up over the cyclone fence, headed for the supply wagon. It was ninety-five degrees out, wet July heat in lower Alabama, but after the hold, it felt good, almost cold. Goose bumps rose lightly on my skin.

Wishbone got off on razzing me. White kid, sixteen, owner's nephew, gone with the summer anyhow. I was his wet dream. We had worked together for a week last summer, my first time on a welding crew, and even then he had no patience for me. He ignored me for the whole week, just looked away whenever I spoke, concentrated on the skittering sparks and pretended I wasn't there. The cigarette runs were a new addition, but I didn't mind so much. Probably, he wouldn't have roughed me up, if I had refused to play along. He would have been fired, maybe jailed, and he knew it, but I wasn't taking any chances.

Summers at the shipyard were a family tradition. Learn the value of a dollar by working hard for it, that sort of thing. I'd drag myself home in the evenings, caked with filth, feeling drained empty, like I'd spent the day donating blood, and there my sister would be, fresh and blonde and lovely, stretched languorously on the couch in front of the television. She'd have on white tennis shorts and maybe still be wearing her bikini top. She spent her summer days reading by the pool, her nights out with one boy or another. She had tattooed a rose just below her belly button by applying a decal and letting the sun darken the skin around it.

"Give me the fucking remote," I'd say.

"Blow me."

She was eighteen, off to the university in the fall. Fifty-one days, I'd tell myself, that's all. It was usually evening by the time I got home and the last of the daylight would be slanting in through the banks of long windows, making everything look dreamy and slow. My sister would yawn and change the channel just to show me she could.

"I'm gonna sit down now, Virginia, and take off my boots and socks," I'd say. "You have until I am barefoot to hand it over or I will beat you like a rented mule."

She would smile pretty, adjust her position on the couch so she was facing me, draw her smooth knees up to her belly, get comfortable. She'd yell, "Mo-om," stretching the word into two hair-raising syllables, "Mom, Ford's acting tough again."

Gerald brought a monkey book to the shipyard, smuggled it in under his coveralls, and the two of us sat around on a break flipping through it. He was an older man, nearing fifty, his dark skin drawn tight over his features, worn to a blunt fineness. He had been working for my uncle almost twenty years. Wishbone lay on his back with his fingers linked on his chest, washed in the rectangle of light that fell through to us. He owned the traces of breeze that drifted down through the hatch. I had the book open across my knees, a droplight in one hand, my back against the bluish-white wall. Gerald was kneeling in front of me, watching for my reaction.

"See there?" he said. "See where it says about spider monkeys make the best pets?"

He reached over the book and tapped a page, leaving a sweaty fingerprint. I flipped pages, looking for the passage that he wanted, past capuchins and Guerezas with their skunk coloring, past howler monkeys and macaques, until I came to the section on spider monkeys. I said, "Okay, I got it."

"Read it to me," he said.

I cleared my throat. "Spider monkey, *Ateles paniscus,* characterized by slenderness and agility. They frequent, in small bands, the tallest forest trees, moving swiftly by astonishing leaps, sprawling out like spiders, and catching by their perfectly prehensile tails. Their faces are shaded by projecting hairs, blah, blah, blah, ten species between Brazil and central Mexico . . ." I skimmed along the page with the droplight. "Okay, here we go. They are mild, intelligent, and make interesting pets. There it is, Gerald."

I tried to hand him the book, but he pushed it back to me.

"Look at the pitcher," he said. "Look at those sad faces."

In the middle of the page was a close-up photograph of two baby spider monkeys. Gerald was right about their faces. They did look sad and maybe a little frightened, their wide eyes full of unvoiced expression, like human children, their hair mussed as if from sleep, their mouths turned down slightly in stubborn monkey frowns.

"Don't nobody got a monkey," Gerald said.

"Michael fucking Jackson got a monkey," Wishbone said.

We turned to look at him. He hadn't moved, was still stretched in the light, legs straight as a corpse. I had thought he was asleep. Gerald said, "Michael Jackson's nobody I know."

"Michael Jackson has a *chimpanzee*, Wishbone," I said. "There's a difference."

Wishbone sat up slowly, drew in one knee, and slung his arm over it. He looked handsome, almost beautiful in the harsh sunlight, his eyes narrow, his smile easy, perspiration beaded on his dark face. He looked so mysterious, just then, I thought that if I could catch him in the right light, strike a match at an exact moment, I would see diamonds or something beneath the surface of his skin.

He got to his feet, walked over, and squatted in front of me. He snatched the book from my hands. "The food of the spider monkey is mainly fruit and insects." Wishbone enunciated each word carefully. He winked at Gerald, then leaned toward me until his face was close enough to mine that I could feel his breath on my cheeks. "In certain countries, their flesh is considered a delicacy." He closed the book and passed it to Gerald without taking his eyes from me. He rooted around under his coveralls, found what he was looking for, and dangled it in front of me. "You know the routine," he said, an empty cigarette pack between two fingers.

I took my time on Wishbone's errand. He hadn't given me a countdown so I thought I'd at least make him wait a while for his nicotine. The shipyard was on skeleton crew since we lost the navy contract—four hundred people out of work at my uncle's company alone—and the *Kaga* was one of only three ships in for repairs, leaving seven dry docks empty, rising up along the waterfront like vacant stadiums. I wandered into the next yard over, yard five, thinking about Gerald's monkey. I wondered if Wishbone could actually get it for him or if that was just talk. I hoped he could for Gerald's sake. Cruel to lead him on. I had this picture in my head of Gerald at home in an easy chair, the television on in front of him and this spider monkey next to him on the arm of the chair, curling its tail around his shoulders. It was a nice picture. They were sharing an orange, each of them slipping damp wedges of fruit into the other's mouth.

I could hear the lifting cranes churning behind me, men shouting, metal banging on metal but yard five was still and quiet. Dust puffed up beneath my steps. The infrequent wind made me shiver. Two rails set wide apart, used for launching ships, ran down to the water's edge and I balanced myself on one and teetered down the slope to the water. A barge lumbered along the river with seagulls turning circles in the air above it.

When I was nine years old, my parents took me to the launching of a two-hundred-foot yacht, the *Marie Paul,* built here for a California millionaire. My family had been invited for the maiden voyage, and we mingled with the beautiful strangers under a striped party tent, which sheltered a banquet of food and champagne and where a Dixieland band fizzed on an improvised stage in the corner. There were tuxedos and spangled cocktail dresses along with the canary-yellow hard hats that my uncle required. The women from

California wore short dresses, dresses my mother never would have worn, exposing tan and slender legs that seemed to grow longer when they danced.

One of these women proclaimed me the cutest thing in my miniature tuxedo and hard hat. She hauled me away to dance, my mother shooing me politely along despite my protests. We did the stiff-legged foxtrot that Mother and I did at home, the only dance I knew. "Loosen up, baby," the woman said, stepping away from me after only a few turns. "Dance like you mean it." She shimmied around me, overwhelmed me, the rustle of her dress and swish of her hair, her hands slipping over my arms and shoulders, her perfume and warm champagne breath, her brown thighs gliding together, her exposed throat and collarbone. This woman did the christening, shattering a bottle of champagne on the prow. The *Marie Paul* was the most magnificent thing I'd ever seen, with a sleek stern and muscular bow, like a tapered waist and broad chest. It was polished incandescent white with a swimming pool at the rear, a helicopter pad on the topmost deck, and four Boston Whalers to serve as landing craft strapped to the foredeck and covered with purple tarp. Workmen on overtime scurried in its shadow, double-checking. My dance partner was tiny beneath its bulk.

Ships are launched sideways, set on giant rollers and drawn down the tracks with heavy cable. When that one hit the water and careened to starboard, sending up a tidal wave of spray, I thought she would go under, that she would keep rolling, slip beneath the slow, brown water and go bubbling to the bottom. I screamed in panic and shut my eyes. My mother pulled me against her leg and said, "It's all right, Ford, honey. Look, it won't sink. See, it's fine." The *Marie Paul* found her balance, came swaying upright, thick waves rushing away from her on both sides, as if drawn ashore by our cheering. Tugboats motored in, like royal attendants, to push her out to deeper water.

I met my uncle on my way back from the supply wagon. He was giving three Japanese men a tour of the yard, all of them in business suits and yellow hard hats. When he spotted me, he yelled my name and waved me over. I stashed Wishbone's cigarettes in my pocket.

"I'd like you gentlemen to meet my nephew," my uncle said, slapping my shoulder. "He's learning the business from the ground up."

I wiped my palms on my coveralls and shook the hands that were offered. Each of the men gave me a crisp bow. They wore black leather shoes, recently filmed over with dust. Since last summer, I had grown three inches. I had my uncle's size, now, and both of us towered over them.

"Hard work," the oldest man said. He made his voice stern and gravelly, as if to imply that physical labor was good for you.

"Yes, sir."

"You better believe it," my uncle said. "No cakewalk for this boy."

My uncle was grooming me. He had no children of his own. Money-wise, my old man did all right as well, exploring the wonders of gynecology, but as I had thus far displayed a distinct lack of biological acumen in school, my parents viewed the shipyard as the best course for my future. My father's routine sounded considerably more pleasant, but I didn't argue.

"Ford, these gentlemen own the *Kaga*." My uncle put his hands in his pockets and rocked back on his heels. "They're thinking about letting us build them another one. Wanted to see a work in progress."

"She's a fine boat," I said and they bowed again.

"*Arigatō.*"

Normally, there was a cluster of men dawdling at the supply wagon but there were no customers now. No one wanted to be caught loafing. All around us, men were busy at their jobs—swarming on deck, unloading a hauling truck over by the warehouse—like a movie version of a bustling shipyard. The air had a faint tar smell and was full of wild echoes, the resolute clamor of progress, the necessary bang of making something from nothing. If you stepped back from it a second, weren't sweating in the guts of the thing, it was sort of heartening. You could almost see giant ships growing up out of the ground.

"Well," my uncle said. "Back to the grind, boy."

When I returned to the *Kaga* with Wishbone's cigarettes, I heard voices drifting up from the hold, and I knew that he and Gerald hadn't yet gone back to work. There was an unspoken understanding among the men, a costly one if my uncle got wind of it. The longer a ship stayed in dry dock, the longer you had a job. My first summer at the yard, I was an industrious dervish, anxious to learn, eager to make a good impression. It wasn't long before I figured out why no one wanted me on their crew. If I worked too hard, they kept up, afraid that I might inform the higher powers. These men walked a fine line. The ships had to be repaired in reasonable time, of course, or there would be no business at all, but if they were finished too quickly, it might seem as if fewer men were needed, or the interval before the next ship arrived might be long enough that layoffs became necessary. The work had to be timed perfectly, not too slow or too fast, or the balance would be upset. It wasn't laziness that slowed the work, as my uncle complained, it was fear. Except Wishbone. I don't know what slowed him down. Wishbone wasn't afraid of anything that I could tell.

I took off my hard hat, belly-crawled to the hatch, and hung myself silently over to watch them. Gerald and Wishbone were on their backs with their feet propped against the far wall, passing a joint between them, its glowing tip visible in the semidarkness. They were giggling like stoned schoolboys.

"Whadju tell him?" Wishbone was talking now, holding the joint between two fingers, blowing lightly on the coal. He dragged, offered it to Gerald, but Gerald waved it away.

"I said, 'Yo dumbass, standing on a trip wire and you want me to stay and *talk?*' Boy want somebody to keep him company while we wait for the EOC. Don't explode when you step on it, see. They blow when you step off, get the guy behind you, which in this case is me. I said, 'You crazy as you are dumb.'"

Gerald laughed a little, which got Wishbone started again too. It took a minute for him to get himself back under control. "You leave him?" he said, finally.

"Naw," Gerald said. "I stuck around a while. Guess I'm dumb as he was."

"Shit, Gerald," Wishbone said. "The Nam."

"It wasn't all bad," Gerald said. "Saw my first live monkey in Vietnam."

They stared quietly at the ceiling for a moment. The sun cast a spotlight beam that fell just short of where they lay, and I could see my shadow in the dusty light. I could feel the blood behind my eyes, could smell all those dead fish that had been there before us. I had been thinking about crashing angrily into the hold, doing an impersonation of my uncle, shouting, "Heads are gonna roll around here," and watching them scramble to their feet in panic, but I decided against it. I was already late with Wishbone's cigarettes. I stood and tiptoed away from the hatch. Then, I approached again, saying, "I'm back, fellas. Sorry it took so long," unnecessarily loud, making extra noise, the way you clomp around when coming home to a dark, empty house to give the burglars or ghosts or whatever time to clear out.

When I got home, finally, I walked around the side of the house to the pool, stripping as I went. My sister was stretched on a lounge chair in her American flag bikini, one knee up, and a boy her age was lying on his side on a second chair, watching her, two sweating glasses of Coke on the table between them. I must have been a strange sight in my boxer shorts, my body pale from hours below deck, forearms and face smeared with sweat and grime, like an actor in blackface only partly painted. They looked up when I passed, and Virginia started to say something, but I didn't give her a chance. I plunged into the clear water, cutting off the sound of her, and let myself glide, rubbing dirt from my arms and cheeks as I went, leaving a distinct, muddy trail in the water, like a jet stream. I floated to the surface in the deep end and hovered there, belly down like a drowned man, until I had to take a breath. The water was pure, cold energy on my skin.

"Mom's gonna kill you for not washing first," Virginia said.

"Mom's not gonna find out, is she." I paddled to the shallow end and stood looking her in the eyes. The pool was chest deep at this end, and my body felt almost weightless in the water.

"She might."

"She won't," I said.

I turned from her, convinced my point had been made. From the pool, our backyard sloped over a neatly cut acre to the sixteenth hole of a golf course. Marking the border between the two was a hedgerow of holly, red berries among the leaves like Christmas decorations. When we were kids, Virginia and I would hide beneath the diving board, submerged to the nostrils like alligators, and wait until a golf ball was shanked into our yard, then we'd swoop down on it and retreat to the pool. We didn't use the balls. They collected like fish tank gravel on the bottom of the pool. We just liked the thrilling mischief of the thing. Now, I could see natty golfers in the fading light and just barely, I could hear the sound of their club faces whisking through the grass, like whispered secrets.

"I'm Art." The boy with my sister was as tan as she was and his hair had been bleached almost white from days in the sun. "You must be the brother."

"You getting laid, Art?" I said without looking at him.

"There's an idea," he said. Virginia socked him in the arm and he winced. He was wearing floral print jams and a bulky diver's watch, one of those that's pressure tested to something ridiculous like six thousand feet.

Virginia said, "That's it. I'm getting Mom."

She stood and padded across the deck toward the sliding doors. I said, "That's a mistake, Virginia," but she kept walking, skipping a little over the hot pavement. She snapped her bikini bottom into place with two fingers as she went. "Bitch," I said. "Dyke, cunt, whore."

"Whoa now," Art said. "You shouldn't talk to your sister like that."

I climbed the four concrete steps from the pool. My body

felt huge and slick and dangerous. It would do whatever I wanted. I walked over to Art, and he stood to meet me. We were almost the same height, and our bodies made a stark contrast, his browned and indolently soft, mine white like hard marble. I leaned into him, our faces inches apart, and gave him an evil wink. "Don't fuck with me, Art," I said. "Just don't." We looked at each other a moment longer before he sidestepped me and followed Virginia into the house.

My sister had a remarkable propensity for never appearing sleep-worn. I didn't know what went on in that bathroom of hers before the lights went out, but she woke each morning in mint condition, emerging from bed as fresh as she went in, no puffy eyes, no crust around the mouth, not a hair mashed out of place by the pillow. She said it was because she never dreamed. But one night, not long after my meeting with Art, I was startled from sleep by something and jerked awake, heart fluttering, thinking I'm late for work, the house is on fire, whatever, to find my sister standing at the window in my room looking out.

"Jesus Christ, Virginia, you scared me shitless," I said. I rolled over to look at the clock. Five-thirty. The night crew at the yard would be getting off any minute. "Get the fuck outta here. I've got an hour left to sleep."

Virginia didn't answer right away. She was wearing her white knee-length nightgown and the light coming through the window made her shape a silhouette beneath the fabric. Her hair was smooth and perfect on her shoulders. My room faced the golf course and I could see morning mist just above the ground.

"What the fuck, Virginia?" I said.

She turned toward me and I knew that she was asleep. Her arms hung loosely at her sides, her fingers curled up a touch. Her eyes were open but as distant as the moon. The world was pulling itself together outside. Sprinklers ticked sleepily on the golf course, the garbage truck ground its way down the street. I pictured Wishbone and Gerald, right then, finishing the first leg of a double shift, coming up from below deck, oiled with sweat, blinking at the dim morning like coal miners.

"Eighty feet," Virginia said.

"What?"

"It has to be eighty feet." Her voice was hushed but firm.

"Okay, Vee, no problem. Eighty feet." I got out of bed and put my hands on her warm shoulders and piloted her back down the hall to her room. She didn't resist and climbed into her bed, a four-poster with an embroidered canopy, when I showed it to her. I couldn't fall back asleep after that. I wondered what my sister was building in her dreams.

Gerald's monkey was on its way. Wishbone had contacted the Jap and the wheels of black market commerce were turning as we spoke. I didn't know whether or not to believe him. It was true that the repairs on the *Kaga* were nearly finished and her crew was filtering back into town, so he could have been in touch with his connection, but I had trouble seeing how a drug dealer from Japan was going to get his hands on a monkey from Brazil. For Gerald's sake, I remained skeptical.

"Wishbone, where's your guy gonna come by this monkey?" I said.

We had finished welding two new plates into the deck and had one more to burn out and replace. The seams from the new plates ran along the floor like tiny, steel molehills. We were kneeling around three sides of a square, burning along white lines drawn in chalk, the heat between us enough to burn the hair from your arms without protection. I could feel the heat pressing against my clothes, could feel it on my tongue when I took a breath.

"What *is* that sound? It's almost like a woman," Wishbone said. "You hear something, Gerald?"

Gerald chuckled beneath his mask. Boot steps echoed above us.

"All I'm saying is, according to Gerald's book, spider monkeys live in Central and South America." The metal beneath the tip of my flame bent and glowed molten orange. "Your guy's not going any-where near South America."

Wishbone shut down his burner and waved at Gerald to do the same. Gerald and I screwed down the nozzles that controlled the gas, reducing the flames to tiny blue pinpoints. Wishbone lifted his mask and breathed in deeply through his nose.

"Listen here, little man, I don't ask questions." He narrowed his eyes at me. "I tell the Jap what I want, and he gets it. Simple as that. Like magic. That's why they call me Wishbone. You trying to dis-courage Gerald? Make him think his wish won't come true?"

At that, my skin prickled. I glanced at Gerald. His mask was still down, the bar of window over his eyes blurred by the heat, but I could tell he was watching us. We were directly beneath the hatch and I could see a block of clear sky above the ship. "Of course not," I said. "I just don't want him to get his hopes up unnecessarily."

"So you think Gerald can't work it out for himself, that it?" Wish-bone said. "He's just some dumb nigger got to be looked after."

"Fuck you, Wishbone."

Wishbone leaned back on his elbows, his temples and neck tracked with sweat. He smiled, then, all the anger in his face suddenly gone, his features smooth with pure delight. That smile was the most terri-fying thing I'd ever seen.

"You hear that, Gerald?" he said. "Nephew's pissed."

"Leave the boy alone, Wishbone," Gerald said, snuffing the flame on his torch and raising his mask. He looked tired. "You know he don't mean no harm."

Wishbone cocked his head and examined me a moment longer, still smiling that amused, unnerving smile. "What Gerald wants, Gerald gets," he said. He fished in his pocket and brought out his cig-arettes. He shook the last three from the pack, snapped two of them at the filter, crumbling the grains of tobacco between his fingers and situated the remaining one between his lips. He said, "What do you think I want?"

For an instant, I thought about saying no, thought about telling

Wishbone to go fuck himself, but I didn't. Something in me resisted the impulse. I don't know whether it was guilt over what Wishbone had said about Gerald or just plain fear or something else entirely, but I dropped my mask and shed my smock and gloves and made my deliberate way up the ladder and into the air.

Outside, the sun was lolling above the crooked tops of the cranes. It was a perfect day for sunbathing. I wondered if Virginia remembered her sleepwalking, remembered the dimensions that troubled her dreams. I walked over to the supply wagon, waving occasionally at one man or another who acknowledged my passing. I knew their faces but rarely did I know their names. Everyone knew me, though. The boss's nephew. The guy that ran the supply wagon saw me coming and had a pack of Winston Reds waiting for me when I arrived.

He smiled and shook his head and said, "Wishbone's daily bread." I forked over the two bucks, thanked him. I turned to retrace my steps across the yard. Right then, the ground rocked and I had to grab the counter for balance. The tremor didn't seem connected to anything, seemed to come from the earth itself, scatter shot and violent, but I saw the source when I turned. For a second, less than a second, I could see the thing, a thick twisting chord of flame, growing up out of the *Kaga* like a vine.

Then it was gone, and I was running hard for the ship, dodging through the wedge of bodies that rushed down the gangplank and away from the explosion. I found Wishbone on deck, four men pinning his arms and legs, telling him, "Lie still, Bone. It's gonna be all right. Don't move." His eyes were squinched tight against the pain, his mouth wide open, his lips chapped looking, but he wasn't screaming. He was naked, his clothes disintegrated by the fire, and his skin was raw and crinkly all over, like the edges of burned paper. Several men were jetting fire extinguishers into the hold, white vapor billowing back, but the fire was already out. That sort of flame was a supernova, here and gone in a flash.

I caught one of the men by his shirtsleeve. "Where's Gerald?" I said. "Let me down there. Gerald's down there. Shut that thing off so we can see him."

He dropped the extinguisher and grabbed my arms.

"You don't wanna see him, son. Believe me."

I let him lead me away from the crowd and sit me down on a spool of heavy cable. My uncle had arrived on the scene by then, and he came over to where I was sitting. "You're okay, Ford?" he said. "What happened? Jesus Christ, your mother would've slit my throat if you'd been down there." He leaned close to me with his idea of a kind expression on his face.

"Gerald wants a monkey," I said.

"Of course he does," my uncle said. "You bet, pal."

My uncle drove me home early from work and dropped me at the front steps. I don't think he was ready to face my mother. I didn't tell anyone at home what had happened, just blew right past them, headed down the hall to Virginia's bed. I climbed in, unwashed, and jerked the covers to my chin. I had this crazy idea that my dreams would be safer there. Virginia came in eventually and said, "What the fuck do you think you're doing?" I didn't answer. Without opening my eyes, I slipped one hand free of the covers and gave her the finger and for some reason, that was enough. I could feel her standing there quietly for a minute or two, watching me. After a while, she said, "You look like a little kid," then she closed the door behind her and left me alone.

To hear Wishbone tell it, Gerald was the smoker. Pack a day at least, must've warned him a hundred times not to smoke around welding lines but he wouldn't listen. Gerald was an old-timer, set in his awful ways. I stood against the wall of my uncle's office a week or so after the accident and waited my turn to speak. My mother was beside me, her hand lightly at my elbow. To my surprise, I felt no anger at Wishbone's lying. The skin on his face was still whitish-pink in places, his sleeves were buttoned to the wrist, covering his scalded arms, and he wore a newborn's light blue knit cap to protect his tender skull. His hands trembled and his eyes were rheumy, his vision blurred, he said, since the accident. He looked weak, vulnerable, afraid, squinting across the conference table at my uncle and the men from the insurance company. I felt sorry for him. I wanted to know what made him think I wouldn't expose him. All the shit he gave me. Maybe he thought I was afraid because he was black or that I was ashamed of being white when he wasn't. Maybe he thought his cigarette run had saved my life and I ought to be grateful, despite everything. But what I wanted to know more than anything was how he survived and Gerald didn't, because for an instant, the amount of time it took to burn away the flammable air, that hold was pure, white conflagration, molten gas, like the center of the sun. Nothing could have lived in there. But here was Wishbone telling these lies right in front of me, burned but alive, breathing in and out like the rest of us when he should have been dead. After things had settled down on the deck that day, I walked over to the hatch and looked in. Two policemen and some emergency personnel were milling around a lumped sheet of blue tarp covering what must've been Gerald's body. It's funny but the stink of all those rotting fish, that death smell, it was gone.

When my turn came to speak, I only had to answer one question—Ford, can you corroborate everything this man has just told us? After but a moment's hesitation, I lied. It wasn't something I'd planned. I'd planned on telling the truth, but in the space of that pause, I thought of Gerald wanting that monkey. He had died believing it would come, hoping for it, and that didn't sound so awful all of a sudden. And I thought of Wishbone, of what good it would do me to ruin his life, what sort of justice would be served. And, strangely, I thought of my sister, so far away from all this, troubled only by rare bad dreams.

"Yes, sir," I said. "He's telling the truth."

I looked at Wishbone, but he wouldn't meet my eyes. He was crying without making a sound. It turned out that he had been standing directly beneath the hatch when he struck the spark that brought the air to life. He had been lifted out by the force of the explosion, shot free of the hold like a cartoon spaceman. One minute, he was standing in a perfect square of yellow light with his friend before him, the next, he was riding a grim column of fire.

Sleeping with My Dog

Holly undressed at the Laundromat. It seemed natural for her to slip out of faded jeans and toss them into the washer with the rest of her load, leaving her in a white ribbed tank top and white panties. She was tan and very blond. I had been watching my own clothes roll in the jet-dry and now I was watching her. It was impossible not to. She turned and met my eyes and smiled, not embarrassed. She was nothing I had ever seen. She was miraculous.

"Are you a mechanic?" she said, mistaking the grout under my fingernails from making mosaics for motor oil. Her voice was a hoarse gift, a delightful surprise.

Holly tells the story of our meeting at dinners, and she told it to her employer when I visited her at work. When she tells it, it is a somewhat different story, more funny, because of the way she describes my facial expression. Her version replaces magic with guile and charm. People laugh and congratulate us on our luck and Holly on her lack of inhibition. Fate is often mentioned.

The two of us, though, don't really talk about the Laundromat when we are alone. It is acknowledged as the place we met, but we do not discuss it. I wonder about that day often, have almost reminded her of it a thousand times but I'm afraid that it will just be an ordinary thing for her, that she slides out of jeans every time she does the wash, displaying her long runner's legs without discrimination. I want it to stay the way I remember it.

I told my brother, Mason, about this one day because I could never keep a secret. My brother, Mason, who is divorced and carries an Old Maid card in his wallet for good luck. It didn't feel properly like a secret, lacked a secret's weight, until I told someone.

"You've lost your balls," he said. "You've positively lost your balls."

Holly moved in with me but that was some time coming. She joked, when I called the first time, that it was against her policy to date a man who didn't have his own washer and dryer. She said that for all she knew I could be a maniac, haunting Laundromats and convenience stores, looking for pretty girls. I said, if that was the case, then why had she given me her number? She didn't have an answer for that. We were quiet a moment. I have a feeling about you, she said.

I live in a hunting cabin in lower Alabama on a lake filled with dead cypress trees. It was abandoned by my grandfather years ago. There is a stillness here, a quiet that I like, that gives no hint that the lake was dug by bulldozers or that the cypress would still be living if not for the imposition of the water.

The quiet helps my work, prevents distraction while I mosaic. Holly laughed, barely managing to stifle it, when I told her what I did for a living.

I said, "I'm trying to perpetuate a dying art."

"That's quite a responsibility," she said.

Really what I do is mosaic picture frames and preshaped vases and ashtrays, whatever, and sell them in craft stores.

I like the meticulousness of it, the slow laying on of cut glass, arranging the pieces according to shape and color and watching the pattern slowly materialize. It's like working a jigsaw puzzle without knowing beforehand how the finished product will look. Then, I cover the whole thing with the gritty, black grout and wipe it away with mineral spirits to reveal the image a second time.

*   *   *

This evening Holly is helping me mosaic. She is home early from work. I showed her, when she moved in, how to cover the shapes with grout, smooth it evenly into the cracks between pieces of glass. If the night is clear and the light lasting, we do this often, sit on the grass on yards of spread newspaper next to the lake. And the mist will rise ghostlike along the water's edge, as if it didn't mind that the lake was man-made—that was in a small way surprising to me—as if it had known that rise forever.

Holly is working with a piece of old flannel shirt, and her lips are pursed at the vase she is holding. She is terrifyingly beautiful like that. Didn't Socrates or someone say that? Beauty is the only truly terrifying thing on earth. But I look at her and think it's good that I'm a little afraid. A nice scared, exhilarating—like being at a movie thriller and your date's fingernails on your arm, suddenly, are more frightening than what's happening on screen. Maybe she is afraid some, too.

"What are you thinking?" I say.

She says, "I want a dog."

"I'm sorry I asked," I say.

The mineral spirits smell wintery.

"I want a dog," she says. "Everything here is either yours or mine. My prints, your furniture. My clothes and your clothes. I want something that can be ours."

"We have joint ownership of all canned goods and Lean Cuisines," I say.

"I mean it," she says. "My family always had dogs. A dog will make this place seem like somebody actually lives here."

"I'm not enough protection for you?" I say, smiling. "Or maybe you'd like me to jump up and lick your face when you come home from work."

She puts the vase down and rubs her face with the back of her hand, leaving a black streak, like athletes' sun guard, under her eye.

"You know what I mean, Banks," she says. "It's too quiet in the woods. Dogs make lots of noise. That reminds me. I have to go on a

New York trip with Alexander next week. It's a step up for me. A permanent traveling position maybe."

Alexander is her boss. Holly is a buyer for a local retail chain. Alexander is grooming her, I hear. She is grinning contentedly. There would be a dog, a boyfriend, and a boss who appreciated her in her life now.

I hear the phone ringing and Holly says, "Mine," and stands and jogs toward the house.

I had been thinking of my brother, Mason, of his divorce and his own dog custody battle. Of Mason on his front porch, beyond drunk, with his chocolate Lab lying across his feet. He was talking to the dog. "She's gone, Brett. Your mama left us high and dry." The dog was quite obviously shattered.

When we were boys our father would sometimes let us sleep out in the kennel, much to my mother's dismay. We had six dogs, three Labs, an Irish setter, and two Boykin spaniels. Mason and I would play Lord of the Dogs, child rulers of a canine kingdom. We could communicate with animals and would pace back and forth in the run on all fours, growling and whining commands to our loyal and devoted subjects. The eight of us would sleep in a pile, indistinguishable, one from the others, in the darkness. The dogs had a smell like that, with Mason and I wedged among them, warm and musty, familiar, safe smelling.

This was a fairly regular event until two of the Labs tore each other's throats out before my father could separate them, when the setter came into season. We had the dogs for years and my father said that he had never, not in all his life, seen anything like it. He got rid of all of them after that. A dog is something to ask of me.

But with the mention of Alexander and New York these thoughts vanish. I picture his wolfish, possessive eyes. His smooth, clean hands on the back of her neck. His suits and shining shoes. When Alexander and I met, he told me he knew his business inside and out, if I knew what he meant. He nodded toward one of the saleswomen in the store.

The screen door to the porch slams shut, and I turn and see Holly standing on the steps. She is wearing jeans and a hunter green V-neck sweater over a T-shirt. Her hands are in her pockets. Her cheek is still smudged with grout.

"Wrong number," she says. "It was somebody for Willy."

A dog is easy. At this moment, I would swallow glass for her.

In the morning, while Holly is at work, Mason and I drive to the ASPCA and pick out a rawboned, year-old golden retriever. He is pale-furred, blond, with hair at his neck the same color as Holly's that fans out like a mane.

The man at the pound says, "He's only been in one day. You're lucky."

Mason says, "Is he purebred?"

"Yep, got papers and everything," the man says. "He won't eat, though. A neighbor called and reported his owner beating him with a two-by-four."

"You know I think this is stupid, right?" Mason says to me.

The dog is thin, yes, his ribs like etchings, but there is something noble about him. In the way he sits, textbook perfect, show-dog straight. When he opens his mouth to let his tongue lag, it looks like he is smiling.

As soon as Holly walks in the door that night and leans down, smiling brightly, to touch him, the dog breaks for the back of the house, paws slipping and skidding on the hardwood. Holly looks hurt. I find him in the bathroom, pressing himself to the wall behind the toilet. He refuses to be coaxed out. I tug at his tail, but it is as tight and desperate as a bowstring.

Holly is sitting on the couch when I return, legs drawn up beneath her, a book pressed against her chest. I haven't turned any of the lights on yet, and the room is shadowy, filling with evening. It looks cold, though it isn't.

"I was told his owner beat him," I say. "It must've been a woman. That's why he ran from you."

"He's a he? He's beautiful," she says, her voice small. "He won't come out?"

I shake my head. I flip on the light, and the shadows are chased to the ceiling. Holly puts her feet down.

"I knew you would get him," she says. "I brought you this for while I'm gone." She hands me the book. *A Hunting Dog's Handbook.* "Teach him some tricks."

"I'm sorry," I say. "You name him."

"He's lovely," she says and stands and walks into the kitchen.

Sunday evening, I drive Holly to the airport, and Alexander is there waiting for us. He takes her carry-on from me and guides her through the metal detector, his hand in the small of her back. Holly says, "I'll miss you. Tell the dog good-bye."

The days without Holly aren't hard for me. I can fill them easily enough. It's the nights that are less than wonderful. The first morning, I wake with the dog sitting leonine and perfect at my side of the bed. I get up and fix both of us breakfast, coffee for me, Alpo for him, but he won't eat until I empty a can of cold chicken soup on his food, a trick my father taught me.

The dog—I name him Pancho, temporarily, until Holly's return—does not leave my side all day. I spread my mosaics out on the porch, working at them halfheartedly, and he stretches out in the grass not ten feet from me and does not move. The sunlight on the glass makes prism reflections on my hands.

"Run around," I tell him. "Go do dog stuff. Dig a hole."

He raises his head, letting his tongue hang out, and looks at me. Behind him is the lake and in it the cypress stumps, standing in the water like ruined columns. Pancho smiles and waits.

I teach him to sit for Fritos. He fetches a wooden coat hanger that I found unoccupied in Holly's closet. Either he has had some experience with these things or Pancho is a genius.

When I turn my back on him to work, he butts his head softly against me, between my shoulder blades, until I free a hand to pet him. I learn to hold a vase between my feet, while I wipe away grout with one hand and scratch Pancho with the other. It is fall and his fur is full of static.

Holly calls at night, and Pancho follows me to the phone. Her voice is full of energy. She has seen Cindy Crawford and Linda Evangasomething at a fashion show. Or she and Alex—it is now Alex— had the most wonderful dinner at the Russian Tea Room. I forget to ask their sleeping arrangements.

I myself cannot sleep. The quiet is pervasive, coming off the lake and filling the air like mist. The bed feels uneven, tilted, without Holly's subtle weight tugging at me from the other side.

I think of letting Pancho into bed with me but decide not to at first. I will let Holly do that if she wants. It will be her decision. And so the door to the bedroom stays shut and for a while the dog gently butts it, then stops. I wonder where he has gone. If he is in the living room in front of the dying fire, like a picture, or in the bathroom across the hall on the tile. I feel guilty and step to the door in the dark, crack it and call his name. He trots past me and hops onto the bed, and I crawl in with him, me under the covers, him on top. I gave him a bath this morning, and he still smells soapy and clean, so I don't worry about Holly noticing fleas in the bed. I just lie there breathing him in, trying to imagine what his name was before me, and thinking that maybe I'll be able to sleep.

But I begin to wonder about Holly in New York, where it is never this quiet, about Alexander, Alex, tapping at her door and telling her he is too excited to sleep. She will be filled with that same warm, liquory tingle of excitement and will let him in.

There are tiny feathers poking through the down comforter where it is worn in places, and I pull them all the way through, making a small mound on the pillow next to me. After a few hours, my eyes adjust completely to the darkness, and I can see the room as if it were daylight. The place on the dresser where her jewelry box usually sits. A bowler hat, hers, on the armchair next to the sweatshirt I wore today. There are times, I think, when no light at all is better than just enough to make a difference.

Alex drove Holly from the airport. I was supposed to pick her up, but they took an earlier flight. That they left early might be a good sign. His headlights draw hieroglyphs in shadow against the wall.

Holly explodes into the room, leaving the door open, and Pancho tightens, growling, and presses against my shins.

"Hello, baby," Holly says to the dog. "I brought you something." She pulls a studded leather collar from her purse and twirls it on her finger.

"I'm not sure that's his style," I say. She leans over the back of the couch and kisses me, then vaults it to sit beside me.

"It's definitely his style," she says. We kiss again, harder, lingering, Holly pressing herself against me, pushing me back against the cushions. Pancho wedges his head between our knees.

"Well," I say, "aren't *you* excited."

"Juiced," she says. "Reborn. This is the ten-thousand-volt Holly. New York is another world."

She pulls away and walks a circle around the couch, stretching, shaking out the airplane kinks. She looks so alive, untouchable, like at the Laundromat with that impossible smile. She stands tiptoe to straighten a bouquet of dried roses she has hung above the door. I swear that where she walks the room gets brighter.

"You hungry?" I say. "I could fix us some dinner."

"Ravenous," she says.

"Stay put," I say. "I'll put something together."

"I want to watch you cook," she says and follows me into the kitchen, hands on my hips, taking wide steps so that her feet fall outside my own. She hops up on the counter.

"Take your clothes off," she says.

"What?" I say. I take a package of spaghetti from the cabinet.

"I want you to cook naked for me," she says. "Maybe just an apron. Parade around the kitchen like a woman in a porno movie."

She is smiling, drumming her nails. Pancho is watching us from the doorway.

"You're awfully frisky," I say. "Should I wear my heels?" I turn on the tap and begin rooting under the sink for a pot.

"I mean it," she says.

I straighten up and look at her. She slips off the counter and leans into me again. The water spatters hotly out of the sink onto my back and my hands, where I'm bracing myself. Pancho rumbles and takes a step into the room.

"It's okay," I tell him. "We're not hurting each other. She's not hurting me."

Holly takes my hand and leads me to the bedroom. She closes the door when the dog tries to follow and says, "Sorry, sweet boy."

I imagine that there is something different about her lovemaking, the way her hips and hands move. Her tongue seems hard and violent in my mouth. Not the same. Asleep later, she kicks the covers and twists on the mattress. For a long time, I try to make my breathing match hers, but I can't for more than a few seconds. Her breathing is impatient and irregular.

I have to stop sleeping with my dog. When Holly leaves the second time, for Los Angeles, I try to resist Pancho's scratching, but eventually I give in and let him sleep with me. I clean dog hair from the blankets every morning. I don't know what Holly would say if she knew, probably nothing good. I tell Mason and he says, "Dogs are dogs and should be treated accordingly." I tell him that I read in some book that the most well-behaved dogs are house dogs, dogs that are comfortable with people. Dogs that sleep with their owners. I don't admit that I made this last part up.

Twice before she left I drove to see Holly at work, leaving Pancho in the back of the truck watching the door expectantly for my return. I would find her in the showroom and lead her away from Alex and the other salespeople, and she told me each time, "No, I will not make love to you in the dressing room." I pretended that I was only teasing, and she smiled and kept her arms firmly between us. The pressure of her arms was at least something.

Pancho and I walk what seems like five hundred miles while she is gone, following the old logging trails through the ginhouse field and Butcher's Field, named when this was still hunting ground. I can't work. Mosaicing makes me restless, is overwhelmingly tedious. Some nights Pancho wakes me with his dreaming. He is on his side on top of the covers, his whole body shaking, paws churning. I wonder if he's having the same dream that I've been having. The one where Holly is coming down the steps of an airplane. It is a propeller plane and the tarmac is wet, like some sentimental forties movie. Humphrey Bogart should be there. And I'm standing on the runway, holding this big ball of light with both hands, waiting to give it to her. I don't know exactly what it is, but I know it's something important.

I call her hotel all the third day, but there is no one around until evening. Alexander answers.

"Alexander, hi. It's me, Banks," I say. "Is Holly there? Have I called your room by mistake?"

We have a bad connection. The static sounds like rushing water.

"Hey there," he says. "Hello from the City of Angels."

I suddenly see him crumpling paper next to the mouthpiece to simulate line interference. But that's ridiculous. I rap the side of my head with my knuckles to stop myself thinking that way.

"No and no," he continues, loudly, "I'm just over here doing some work. Sorry, but I sent Holly on an errand. Boundless energy that girl."

"Oh," I say. "I understand."

He says, "Everything's great here. A little business and a lot of pleasure, if you know what I mean. She's a terrific girl."

Pancho gets to his feet and watches me. Behind him is a bookcase filled with my work. A decorative bowl with a mosaiced daisy in the center. A pitcher done in black and red with a slender handle. It took patient hours to cut glass small enough for that handle. Clay candlesticks in Christmas colors. All the things that I have made.

"Hello?" Alexander says.

"I'm here," I say.

"Holly said the strangest thing to me today," he says. "We were coming back from a lunch meeting and there was one of those daytime moons. You know the kind I'm talking about?"

"Un-hunh." I can see it. The moon white and false-looking in the light. Its surface scarred with dry blue lakes, its edges blurring into the pale sky.

"And she looks me right in the eye and says she wishes she could walk on the moon," he says. "That someday they're going to colonize it up there. Isn't that strange?"

That sounds like something Holly would say. I picture her—I can't help seeing her with him—scanning the sky for an uncommon moon, one hand raised to shade her eyes, drawing a perfect line of shadow across the bridge of her nose.

"Yes," I say, "very."

"Well," he says.

The static evaporates. His voice, saying good-bye, is clear but distant from the mouthpiece. There is a long moment before he hangs up, when I imagine I can just barely hear someone moving in the background.

I call Mason and tell him that I want to get drunk. He takes me to a Western bar that he likes, where they make me take off my baseball cap, even though fully half of the men inside are wearing Stetsons. I wore the hat because I haven't showered since Holly left, and my hair is slick and dirty and stays close to my head.

Mason guides me to a seat at the bar and we watch the dancers, lined up, moving stiffly in unison. They all know the steps. It is an unfortunate combination, the seventies disco lighting, blinking pink and turquoise, and the awkward line dance, a cotillion version of someone's idea of country western dancing.

"You look like shit," Mason says.

"Thank you very much," I say.

"If it's driving you this crazy put an end to it," he says. "I always tell people, if you're worried, you've probably got good reason to be worried. Simple as that."

He knows that I know what he means.

I had the idea that I would have an affair tonight, sleep with someone completely different than Holly. I would find a tall and skinny country girl, all angles to Holly's athletic curves. But what would I do if I found her? I wouldn't know how to begin, wouldn't have anything to say to her or know how to kiss her. Holly has taken all of that from me.

"You've spoiled that dog absolutely rotten," Holly says to me. She is sitting on the couch twisted around to watch me feed Pancho leftover cake and ice cream. The two of us, the dog and I, had a party last night, when I came in drunk, and ate ourselves silly. Holly folds her arms on the back of the couch and rests her chin on them. To the dog she says, "You're ruined, Pancho. I mean it."

He raises his eyes but keeps eating. I made certain to pick up Holly at the airport this time but couldn't think of anything to say in the car. It was the longest hour of my life, but Holly didn't seem to notice and filled my silence easily, it seemed, with stories of Los Angeles. Alex is going to carry Donna Karan this season. They saw Michael Bolton on the sidewalk in West Hollywood. She met a group of ten phenomenally—her word—handsome gay men, handsome as statues, she said. She couldn't understand why they were gay, looking like that. I said maybe they had never seen anything as beautiful as each other. She laughed.

Now she says, "Where have you been the last two nights? I tried to call. I let it ring and ring."

"I don't know," I say. "Maybe I was in the shower. Or outside with the dog."

"It was like midnight when I called," she says. "You two are unnaturally attached."

She smiles and pats the couch next to her for me to sit down. Last night, when she called, I was sitting right where she is sitting. I knew it was her but let the phone keep ringing, twenty, thirty earsplitting rings. It was all I could do not to answer. I wanted to vomit. I wanted her to wonder.

The phone rings now, and I nearly jump out of my skin.

"Is Willy home?" The voice says. A woman's voice.

I tell her she has the wrong number but she doesn't believe me. She reels off my number and I say, "Yes, that's right but there's no Willy here."

"Just put him on, Arthur," she says. "This is Arthur, isn't it?"

"No," I say.

Holly smiles and shakes her head. She says, "Hang up on 'em." She makes a phone with her hand, thumb as earpiece, pinky mouthpiece, and slams it on an imaginary receiver.

I don't hang up. I can hear music playing softly in the background. Jazz. The woman sounds a little drunk.

"Look, Arthur," she says, "I haven't talked to him in a week."

"I'm sorry about that," I say.

"Just tell him that I called. Please, Arthur. Make sure he knows that I called," she says.

"I'll tell him," I say. "I promise."

I hang up and cross the room to Holly. She drapes her arm over my shoulders and sags against me. We watch the fire play.

"You've been sleeping with Alexander," I say.

"Don't be silly," she says. I expected a reaction, but there is nothing. She is still soft and warm against me, relaxed, innocent, fingertips brushing the back of my neck. The dog circles, then curls up in front of us, between the coffee table and our feet. This could be so right. It could be.

"Let's go to bed," Holly says.

"I'm not tired," I say. "You go on."

"I'll put up with this forever," she says. "If you want me to."

Pancho scrambles to his feet, suddenly, and rushes to the window barking. He has the deep, booming bark of a dog twice his size. Its sound fills the room, like a gunshot, and its force causes him to bounce and hop with each report.

Holly puts a hand on my cheek and turns my face toward her. She kisses me, but I don't open my mouth. The dog stops barking but doesn't leave the window. Holly takes her shoes off, pushing each one loose with the toes of the other foot. She stands and pads gently to the bedroom. For a while, I pretend that Holly will come back and stand in the doorway and smile the way she did at the Laundromat, as if everything, all of this, were perfectly natural. But I don't believe that it is.

I go over and crouch next to the dog, shading my eyes so I can see past our reflections, trying to see what spooked him. There isn't anything out there that I can see, just night. In the faint moonlight, I can make out the drowned cypress trees looming up from the water. I try to remember if I have made Holly any promises. Or she me. I can't remember.

Amelia Earhart's Coat

When she was in the fourth grade, Hettie saw her father kissing Amelia Earhart. Hettie wasn't supposed to be at home, was supposed to be down the beach swimming with her mother and the Fitzgeralds, but she wasn't. She was cutting through the dining room on her way to the wide balcony that faced the ocean. She was angry at her mother for embarrassing her and had a sketchy plan to rest her elbows on the stone railing, her chin in her hand, and stare wistfully out at the ocean, like a prisoner in a story musing of home. But this was better. Both sets of French doors were open and the sail-white curtains were billowing back into the room, and beyond the doors, in dreamy flashes because of the waving curtains, she saw Amelia Earhart in her father's arms.

Not fifteen minutes before, Hettie had been wading in the shore-break with Baker Fitzgerald. She couldn't actually swim, because she had a cast on her arm. Baker was a year older, and they went to the same school in the city. He had jabbed a finger over Hettie's shoulder. "Ahoy," he said, "a white whale." Hettie had turned to look and seen her mother in a bathing cap, floating on her back in the water. Her arms were spread like flabby wings and her skin was pale and doughy-looking, bunched beneath her swimsuit. Her lips were blue with cold. She was as bloated as a drowned man. Hettie threw a fistful of sand at him and stalked off down the beach. Her mother hadn't seen her leave.

Hettie took an apple, now, from the crystal bowl on the dining table and sat in her father's place. Her father was the most handsome man she knew. A Panama hat was perched on his head, cocked back to show his dark widow's peak, and he had snappy little creases at the corners of his eyes and mouth. He was so tall that he had to stoop to kiss Amelia Earhart and she had to lift herself on tiptoe, her round, bare heels coming out of her shoes, to reach his lips.

Hettie was reading a book that summer in which spies had lived with deaf people for a year to learn how to read lips. Hettie was practicing. She watched her father's mouth moving, then Amelia Earhart's. She shifted the hard apple from hand to hand, thumping it against her cast, and concentrated on their lips. Unless she was mistaken, Amelia Earhart said to her father, "Peter Saxacorn, I love you more than anything in the world."

This was Rye, New York, March 1937. A line of magnificent houses stretched along the beach like gracious actors preparing for a bow. The air was still wintry, but that didn't stop summer residents from reclaiming their houses, bringing servants out from the city to open the windows, clean the linens, scrub the bitter salt smell from the floors. Everyone in Rye knew that Amelia Earhart was preparing to leave soon on another flight, this one around the world. Hettie knew everything about her. Born in Atchison, Kansas. College at Columbia. Summer school at Harvard, where she became friends with Hettie's mother. She had already flown with Wilmer Stultz and Louis Gordon across the Atlantic, across the very ocean that stretched grayly away from the beach where Hettie's mother had humiliated her. She had piloted a plane all on her own along the same route, setting a new speed record for the crossing: 13 hours, 30 minutes. And again, two years later, she had flown nonstop from Mexico City to New York—14 hours, 19 minutes—another record. She wasn't just the fastest woman; she was the fastest anybody.

One thing Hettie could say in her mother's favor was that she had brought Amelia Earhart into their lives. They were friends before Hettie was born, when her mother was still beautiful. Hettie had seen pictures of them together. Boston, against a plain brick wall. Their hair bobbed short, like schoolboys, their slender calves and narrow ankles below knee-length dresses.

When Miss Amelia—that's what Hettie called her—would come to dinner, she would say, "Your mother was a wild one, Hettie. Every boy from Annapolis to Princeton was after her." She would flash a wide, tipsy smile and laugh out loud like a man. "But Peter was the lucky one." Here, she would touch the backs of Mr. Saxacorn's fingers. "They were the most beautiful couple. The envy of the known world."

He'd say, "I'm a lucky man," and draw his hand away.

"Poor Peter," Hettie's mother would say. "I'm sorry I can't be beautiful for you anymore. I never bounced back from carrying you, Hettie. I gave you all my beauty in that delivery room."

Hettie's mother was English and her voice squeaked when she was drunk. She'd try to catch Hettie and pull her into her lap, but Hettie was too old for that and besides, the thought of being born made her cringe. Hettie would skip away, stay just out of her reach. Her mother was too heavy and too drunk to catch her.

"You're still the most beautiful woman I know," her father would say and his dishonest kindness made Hettie love him more.

Now, lying in her bed, the dampness from her bathing suit soaking into the sheet beneath her, Hettie remembered Amelia Earhart's hand on her father's. She was glad for him. Maybe they had always been in love. Her mother would be angry when she discovered the wet sheets, sandy from her feet, but Hettie didn't care. She closed her eyes and she was in a Lockheed Vega with her father and Amelia Earhart. They were flying above Rye on a mad dash for Mexico City. Amelia was at the stick. The massive houses scrolled by beneath them one by one until they came to the house of Charles Putnam, Amelia's husband, where they swooped down for a closer look. He was standing on his own balcony looking up at them, smiling sadly.

He raised his drink; he was sorry to see Amelia go but he, unlike Hettie's mother, understood that you can't stand in the way of true love. They dipped a wing in salute, then looped away from him into the sky. A voice behind Hettie said, "Ahoy, a white whale." She turned around and her father was gone. In his place sat Baker Fitzgerald, his skin already beginning to tan, his hair the color of a wedding ring. He was pointing out the window and she followed his finger with her eyes until she saw a surfacing whale, massive and sickly white with red-rimmed eyes and algae growing on its back, water rushing from its exposed flanks. Amelia said, "Hold on tight, Hettie," and they dove again. The engines howled. Baker's arms slipped around her waist. Gunfire broke the water like raindrops.

Hettie opened her eyes, walked over to the full-length mirror. She studied herself close up. Her hair sticky from the salt in the wind, the constellation of freckles across the bridge of her nose. She stepped back and turned sideways, hiding her cast against her body. She had no figure yet, was lean and tall like her father, but that didn't mean she wouldn't ever have one. There was hope for her yet. She would just be sure not to have children.

Her parents were having a party tonight and everyone would be there. The Blackfords and the Duponts, the Marchands and the Exleys. Neville what's-his-name—the diplomat who had served with Hettie's grandfather in the foreign service—he would be there, too. Amelia Earhart would come with her husband. Hettie wondered what it was like for her father and Amelia Earhart, having to hide their love. Having to be nice to her mother and Mr. Putnam, having to kiss each other on the cheek, when what they wanted to do, Hettie imagined, was go running up the stairs and fall into each other's arms. She ached for them.

Tonight, her mother would dress her up in one of the frilly, little-girl dresses with a low waist. She would put a bow in her hair and parade her around the house a few times to greet the guests, before banishing her to her room for the duration of the party. Everyone would ask about her cast, and her mother would tell the story for her, would get it all wrong. Hettie was running from her awful parents, her mother would say. She'd been sent to her room and was trying to escape. She would tell the story dozens of times, maybe changing it a bit once in a while, and everyone would laugh. But that wasn't it at all. Hettie always obeyed her father. She wouldn't have run from him. She had been standing at her open window on the second floor looking at the smaller houses across the cockleshell road, white as bones, and had suddenly realized that she *could* jump. She could ease out onto the sill and hurl herself off, give herself up to the air. And that's exactly what she did. It was as if she couldn't stop herself. It had been the most thrilling thing she had ever done, worth all the pain, when she pitched forward on the grass and snapped her wrist, worth the miserable, persistent itching. Only Amelia Earhart could understand something like that.

Hettie's mother had big plans for her cast. Just that morning, sprawled on a beach chair, like something washed up from the sea, she had said, "Hettie, how does this sound? We'll paint your name with nail polish on your cast. I'll do it in calligraphy. I learned calligraphy in school and I haven't tried it in years—It'll be smashing—and we'll tie a bow around it, a blue one like your dress. What do you say?"

Calligraphy. What a useless talent. Nothing at all like lip-reading or disguise. Nothing at all like flying a plane. Even now, Hettie heard the servants downstairs moving furniture to make a dance floor, the caterers setting up. From her window, she could see sofas and end tables being carried across the neat lawn and loaded into trucks to be carted away. They would be stored for the night and returned in the morning. Hettie stripped out of her bathing suit and changed into dry clothes. She crept to the head of the stairs and listened for her mother. She could hear her voice, directing the caterers, drifting in from the beach. Her mother wouldn't want her wandering off so close to the party.

"Hettie, what are you up to?" Her father's voice behind her.

She turned to find him leaning out of the bathroom, just head and shoulders, hair slicked back with water. The left side of his face was smeared with shaving cream, the right smooth and clean. He had a cigarette between his lips. She stepped over to him on tiptoe and kissed his cheek. She wanted to smell him, that lime and soap smell with the smoke all mixed in. She stepped back, winked, and pressed a finger to her lips. He said, "I get it. Secret mission. Mum's the word. Aye, aye, captain." Her father had been a navy man.

"Close your eyes," she whispered and he did as she asked.

"Don't hurt me," he said, eyes squinched shut, a pencil line of smoke drifting up from between his lips.

Hettie nicked a cigarette from the pack on the ledge of the sink and trotted back to the landing, waited until two workmen passed carrying a long striped sofa, then dashed down the stairs and threw herself into the cushions, pressed herself flat. They wobbled, a moment, under her weight but didn't stop. She got off at the back of the truck, thanked them for the ride, and headed off down the road toward the Fitzgeralds'. Maybe Baker would want to share her cigarette.

She knocked on the kitchen door and was met by a colored woman who sat her down at the kitchen table and asked her to wait while she went to fetch Baker. The kitchen was immaculate, smelled of bleach. Baker came in without the colored woman and stood in the middle of the room. He said, "Whaddaya want?"

She held the cigarette between the knuckles of her middle two fingers and raised her eyebrows. He found a box of matches in the drawer. They sat on the back steps and smoked, passing the cigarette between them.

"Don't you want to take this down to the beach or something?" Hettie said.

"Don't worry. No one'll come out. They're all getting ready for your party."

He dragged and looked away, squinting toward the sunset. Very handsome. He didn't cough. Beyond the line of scraggly trees, the sun was flaring out, the sky bleeding light. Hettie said, "I'd still rather be on the beach. My mom'll kill me."

"I can't." He passed her the cigarette.

"Why not?" Hettie said.

When he didn't answer right away, she asked again.

"Breece Marchand is back home," Baker said. "My parents won't let us out alone after dusk. They're worried that he'll, you know, try something."

"We could handle him," Hettie said, but she didn't press it. She knew about Breece Marchand. She could picture him. Broad, stupid forehead, tall with slumped shoulders. Breece was almost ten years older than her and Baker. He was the boy that had attacked—her mother's word—Baker's older sister. Hettie didn't know exactly what that meant—With a knife? His bare hands? Something else?—but it sounded sinister enough. She knew that the police had come, and he had been sent "away" for a while. She remembered her parents having whispered arguments at the kitchen table about what had happened. She scanned the tree line for dark figures. Then said, "What's he look like now, so I'll know if I see him? Does he look different? What exactly did he do, so I can tell the police if there's trouble?"

Baker started to answer, then stopped. An odd, closed look came over his face. He snatched the cigarette and took a long drag, the ash crackling, then flicked it off into the dunes. He said, "We saved your ass in the war."

"What the hell are you talking about?"

"If not for our boys, the Kaiser would have whipped you limeys for sure."

"I'm no limey," Hettie said. "My father was in the navy."

"Your mother's from England," Baker said. "The English are notoriously fat."

"Not me." Hettie stood. She thumped her chest with her cast. "I was born and raised in Atchison, Kansas."

She ran down the steps and kept running. It was almost dark and night was bringing cold. The trees were full of dangerous shadows all the way home.

Hettie skidded through the open front door and slammed into her mother, her face pressing into her mother's breasts, her hands, in an effort to stop herself, digging into her mother's spongy stomach. She wrenched herself backward against the wall. Her mother said, "Good Lord, child, slow down. You nearly flattened me." She touched a hand to her chest, took a moment to collect herself. "We've got to get you dressed." Hettie knew there was no use arguing.

She let herself be led upstairs and sat on the bed, hiding the damp impression her body had left on the sheets, while her mother ran her a bath. Her mother waited while she undressed, watched her, made certain she was installed in the steaming water, before she went downstairs for a glass of wine. "I'll be right back," her mother said in warning.

Hettie hated being bathed—*children* were bathed—but she had no choice. She couldn't even wash herself because of the cast. Her mother had told her that her skin would go rotten beneath the plaster if she let it get wet. She pictured her decayed arm, saw it like the soggy driftwood that washed up on the beach. She could break it with her fingers, peel away soft splinters, as easy as pulling cooked chicken from the bone. Part of her, a small part, wanted to sink the cast, to hold her arm underwater, soak it through, to see if what her mother told her was true.

Her mother returned carrying a washcloth and her wine. The wine she set on the edge of the tub, the washcloth she soaped and used to scrub Hettie, head to foot, her calves, the insides of her thighs, her stomach and chest, her neck. She washed her hair. Hettie sat frozen, waiting for it to be over. She was too humiliated to open her eyes. When the washing was done, her mother had Hettie step from the tub to be dried. "Keep your cast over your head," she said. Hettie did as she was told. She could feel the water, cooling now, running down her arm, over her rib cage, could feel her mother's hands pressing the towel against her.

"Can't I dry myself?" Hettie said.

"You wouldn't have to suffer so, if you weren't such a daredevil."

Her mother waited while Hettie tried on dresses, a fourth, a fifth, finally coming back to the second, light blue, ankle-length, with a bow of darker blue satin at the waist. Her mother's wineglass had long been empty.

"We don't have time to do your cast, Hettie," she said. "If you hadn't disappeared all afternoon . . . But I have to get ready myself."

Hettie tried hard to look disappointed.

Downstairs, Hettie could hear the band warming up, random cymbal rattles, occasional toodling notes, and in between, the clatter of dishes. She couldn't help but feel excited before her parents' parties. And Amelia Earhart would be arriving soon. Amelia Earhart, the woman who would fly her twin-engine Lockheed, called the "Flying Laboratory," not just across the ocean but around the world. After a false start in Oakland, not a month before—the plane did a ground loop, turned uncontrollably before it was ever airborne—she told reporters, "If we don't burn up, I'd like to try again." Hettie had saved the newspaper clipping.

She wondered if her father was excited, too, if he was plotting a secret rendezvous, right under her mother's nose. Hettie went to the window to watch for cars. Night had settled in, by then, and candles, sheathed in white glass, lined the walkway. It wasn't long before the guests began to arrive, smiling faces streaming up the front stairs and into the house, and the band started up. The sound from below, music mixed in with all the voices, caused a tightness in Hettie's chest, like she was sitting on the lid of a boiling pot. Finally, Hettie saw George Putnam's ragtop Cord roadster easing off the road a bit away from the house, saw him in the light of the headlights—tiny round glasses glinting, dark overcoat—walk around the front of the car and open Amelia's door. Hettie ran to her door and stood behind it, waiting for her mother to call her downstairs. She imagined her father at his own door just down the hall, trembling with anticipation. How romantic, Hettie thought.

"Hettie, come down now. Miss Amelia's here to see you." Her mother's voice, at last, from the bottom of the stairs.

Hettie found her mother and Amelia Earhart standing in the

foyer, laughing. Amelia was beautiful in a black mink coat and the softest-looking midnight blue dress with a low-slung collar. She was wearing a strand of pearls, looped three times around her neck. The room was a dazzle of light. They turned to her and Amelia said, "Hettie, come here. Show me your cast."

Hettie trotted over and gave her a hug. Amelia crouched beside her and held the cast gingerly, as if it were the most valuable thing in the world.

"I jumped from the second-story window," Hettie said.

Amelia pressed her lips together in appraisal. Hettie's mother said, "An escape attempt, Millie."

"No," Hettie said, quickly. "That's not it."

Her mother laughed. "Then what was it, dear?"

"I just wanted to," Hettie said. She searched Amelia's face for a better explanation. Her hair was short and full of curls, brown with streaks of blonde that Hettie thought looked like moonlight.

"And so you did it, didn't you," Amelia said. "It's a badge of honor, then."

Hettie had known that she would understand. Her mother laughed again and said, "Please, Millie." Then to Hettie, "Darling, will you take Miss Amelia's coat to the guest room."

She slipped out of her coat, draped it over Hettie's arms, and thanked her. Hettie said, "I know my father is looking forward to seeing you."

Amelia Earhart looked at her curiously, head cocked, a slight smile on her lips.

"I'm looking forward to seeing him, too, dear."

Hettie carried the mink down the hall. The bed was already piled high with furs, but the mink was the most beautiful coat she had ever seen. She held it at arm's length and shook it out, the way she had seen her mother do at Saks. Something heavy shifted in the pocket. She slipped her arms into the cool, silk-lined sleeves, closed her eyes, wrapped the coat around her. She let it envelop her, pushed her fingers through the fur, pressed her face into the collar, smelled the perfume and cigarettes there. She couldn't believe how soft it was. It tickled, made her cheeks tingle. She imagined Amelia Earhart wearing this coat in her father's arms, her father rubbing his smooth cheeks on her shoulder. The music from the other room didn't quite reach her, dissolved in conversation on the way and arrived in scattered notes.

Hettie let her hands drift down her sides, into the pockets, and her eyes snapped open. Her right hand closed over something metallic. She thought, even before she brought it out, that it was a pistol. She lifted it gingerly, held it with both hands in front of her face and blinked at it. Along the barrel she read, *O. F. Mossberg & Sons/New Haven, Conn. U.S.A.* She had never seen a pistol before, not counting Civil War relics at the museum. She closed one eye and squinted down the squared barrel. She could see four tubes, like smaller barrels, inside, but she couldn't tell if there were any bullets. Hettie palmed the gun, tested its weight. She wondered why Amelia would be carrying a pistol. Was she in danger? Was she afraid that someone was trying to sabotage her flight around the world? Hettie's heart jumped. She could hear blood hissing behind her ears. Hettie thought suddenly that Amelia Earhart was going to kill her mother. She was going to take this gun, this hard gun in Hettie's palm, and creep up behind her mother and pull the trigger and run off with her father to Mexico. She could hear the pop and see the muzzle flash, like in the movies, could imagine her mother's body crumpling heavily to the floor, could almost smell the acrid gunpowder smoke lingering in the air. Hettie's mouth was desert dry. She thought of warning her mother, she had to do *something*. Her father wouldn't agree to a murder plan. He wouldn't let it happen, would he? The idea terrified her, but she didn't want to stand in the way of his happiness, didn't want to be the one to keep them apart.

Right then, there was a knock at the door, and she heard a squeaky "Hettie? Are you there?" Her mother, already nearing drunk. The door swung open and her mother appeared, leaning on the knob. Without thinking, Hettie darted under her arm and raced through the house, dodging guests, slipping through greedy hands, hearing voices say, Easy there, little girl. Slow down now. You'll break your other arm if you're not careful. The makeshift ballroom was brilliant with noise. Hettie didn't stop. She tore through the double doors and out onto the beach, where torches on metal stands flickered in the breeze. She would take the gun away from the house, until she'd had time to figure out what to do. She kicked out of her shoes and kept running, her feet throwing clumps of sand behind her. She ran until she was far enough down the beach that the light from the house was a distant glimmer and only then, doubled-over, panting in the sand, her broken arm throbbing vaguely, did she remember that she was still wearing Amelia Earhart's mink coat.

The dark ocean was beside her, waves breaking as straight and white as lines of chalk on a blackboard. A chill wind snapped American flags up and down the beach. Hettie was alone, but she knew that someone would be along shortly to look for her. Not in a million years would her mother leave her alone on the beach at night with a gun and a stolen mink. Maybe her father would come looking with Amelia Earhart—she would, after all, be wondering about her things—and they would find her and tell her everything. They would sit with her in the sand and tell her not to worry, everything was going to be all right. They wouldn't leave her when they made their break. The plane had room enough for three.

In the distance, away from her parents' house, she could see a bonfire dancing, shadow figures moving in its light. She walked in that direction, wrapped the coat close about her against the cold. She stopped well short of the fire. Three boys, college-aged, were gathered around it—one sitting, two standing—passing a bottle between them. They didn't see her standing there, just kept moving and talking in the orange glow. She couldn't make out what they were saying so she tried to read their lips, but the light was strange and blurry and she couldn't see them well enough to understand. Hettie felt she was witnessing something secret. She crept forward until she could hear them, their voices intent and serious. She didn't make a sound.

"So you're saying to me, let Mussolini *have* Ethiopia," one of the standing boys said, the skinny one. "Just let him roll an army into someone else's country and have it. We can't *do* that." His voice was high-pitched and whiny.

"Why not?" This from the seated boy. He took a sip from the bottle, tossed a little sand into the fire, dimming it briefly. The light played eerily on his face. Hettie couldn't take her eyes off of them.

"Whaddaya *mean* why not?" Hettie thought he sounded like he was holding his nose. She had to stop herself from laughing at him. "Are you some kinda pacifist? We can't just let him have it. Didn'ya read Salassie's speech in the paper?"

"Salassie's a spade. It's a spade country. I say he's welcome to it."

The boy standing closest to Hettie, the one who hadn't spoken, suddenly snapped his head in her direction and said, "Jesus Christ, you scared me half to death, standing there like a ghost. What're you doing? Come over where I can see you."

Hettie said she was sorry and stepped into the light. She was glad to be noticed, grateful to be invited into their circle. She hoped the coat made her look older.

"Who is it, Breece?" The sitting boy again.

"It's a little girl in a mink coat." He smiled warmly at her.

Breece, he'd said. Breece Marchand. Hettie didn't move any closer.

"I'm not little," she said. "I've got a gun."

"Hey, Richie," the whiny one said, laughing. "The little girl's gotta gun."

"I heard her, moron," Richie said. "She stood right there, where all of us can hear her, and said, 'I'm not little, I've got a gun.' Why do you have to go around repeating things all the time?"

"Be quiet, you guys," Breece said. "You're scaring her."

Hettie drew the pistol from her pocket and held it, trembling, in front of her. This was the boy that had attacked Baker's sister. Hettie didn't know what he had done exactly, but she knew it was something awful, something that couldn't be talked about. She was terrified.

What if he attacked her? Right here on the beach. The others, too. She couldn't stop them, one ten-year-old girl, unless she shot them.

"Jesus, put that thing down," Breece said. "You'll hurt yourself."

He took a step in her direction and she took a step back. She waved the gun at the other two, then brought it back to Breece. She could shoot him, pull the trigger right now, and he would be dead. A breakneck feeling washed over her, the feeling she'd had on the windowsill right before she jumped.

"I know who you are, Breece Marchand," Hettie said. "I know what you did."

"She's *on* to you, pal." The whiny one laughed a little and shook his head. "What the hell's she talking about?"

Richie didn't move or say anything, just watched. Breece showed Hettie his palms and took another step. He didn't look like someone to be afraid of, didn't even look the way she remembered. He looked nice, actually, handsome, short hair, a blue oxford shirt untucked over khaki pants, barefoot. He had tiny, delicate-looking feet for a man. He saw her looking at them and dug his toes into the sand.

"I think she's talking about Delia Fitzgerald," he said.

"*That?* Christ."

"I know what you did," Hettie said.

"Look, little girl, I don't know what you've heard, but you shouldn't be afraid of me. I didn't do anything." He spoke softly, sounding weary, a little embarrassed. "She made it up, the whole thing. I don't know why."

Hettie didn't know what to think. What was it that he was supposed to have done? She kept the gun pointed at him, but she knew she couldn't shoot. The wind whipped up, twisting sparks above the fire. Hettie shivered. Faintly, from way off down the beach, she heard her name. Her father was calling her. She looked at Breece Marchand and their eyes met. He was looking at her strangely, imploringly, as if he didn't want her to go.

Hettie turned, feeling the warmth of the fire leave her face, and ran until she reached her father. He caught her by the shoulders, held her at arm's length and shook her. He said, "Hettie, what on earth is wrong with you? Running off with Amelia's coat. Your mother's worried sick." She dropped the gun and let herself go limp in his hands. He picked it up, still supporting her with one hand, and blew sand from the barrel. "Where did you get this? This is Amelia's gun, isn't it?" he said. "Stupid, crazy woman. Bringing a gun into my house."

Hettie held her father tight around the waist. His chest was warm against her cheek, except for one pinpoint of cold where his tuxedo stud touched her face.

"Don't be angry at her," she said. "Don't let her leave me when you fly off together."

"What do you mean—fly off together?" He picked her up and looked at her face. She was crying, shaking with sobs and the cold.

"I saw you kissing. Don't leave me when you go."

Her father pulled her against him. "Oh, Hettie," he said, his voice gentle, soothing, almost amused. "Hettie." He carried her all the way back to the house.

Two days later, Amelia Earhart left Rye, New York, and she didn't return all summer. She was preparing for her flight around the world. In June, Hettie listened to takeoff reports on the radio. She spread a map on the desk in her room and traced the route in pencil. Miami to San Juan to Caprito to Paramaribo to Natal. From there, across the Atlantic, her third trip, to St. Louis. There was a St. Louis in Africa. Hettie thought that was wonderful. With the trail drawn before her, etched like smoke on the sky, it looked like such a long way to go. Calcutta to Akyab, Bangkok to Singapore. When the plane vanished, disappeared into thin air, between Lea, New Zealand, and Howe Island, Hettie, crying, said to her mother, "You did this," though she couldn't understand how. "You made this happen so they couldn't be together," though she felt, with surprising certainty, that it could not possibly be true.

A Bad Man, So Pretty

Winston got kicked out of military school for smoking dope. He was a big guy, my brother, roped with muscle through his neck and shoulders, but after two months of home cooking in place of barracks' chow, he started to develop a gut, not really flab, more like a knot of tension, like someone had surgically implanted a volleyball beneath the surface of his skin. He stopped wearing his glasses and refused to try contacts, said it would drive him crazy to have something touching his eyeballs all the time. I think he just wanted an excuse to go around with a Clint Eastwood squint. My brother had always been a little left of normal. Instead of just the regular crew cut, he shaved his head bald for military school—Win never did anything halfway—and his hair grew back in tight crow-black ringlets, like an Afro, when before it had been straight and rawhide brown. He looked only vaguely like the person he had been before.

Marshall Military Institute was a two-hour drive from Mobile, stashed away in the scrub pinewoods of lower Alabama, left over from a time when military school was a more fashionable form of education. It was his third high school in four years, enough moving around that, at twenty years old, he still hadn't graduated. Win never moaned about getting shipped away, and he never tried to explain himself when they sent him back. There was a boarding school in New England, where he wrote a paper entitled "Banging My English Teacher or What I Think About When I Should Be Thinking About Samuel Clemens." I don't think his teacher got past the first line, before Win was booked on the next flight home. Then came this New Age place in Colorado—my mother's idea—where student problems were discussed in what they called "powwows." You had to be holding the magic talking stick or something before the group would let you say your piece. Win hated it. It took him almost six months to get rolled. He said they talked you to death out there; they wouldn't get angry, no matter what you did. That is, until the incident with the laboratory cats. Mom still won't let us mention it. Win's biology class had been dissecting stray cats. He broke into the lab and swiped the cats, along with mannequins from the art room, and decorated the campus with them, arranging them in trees, on benches, in the teachers' lounge. It gave me the creeps to think about, dozens of skinned cats, gray and shriveled, perched in the laps of mannequins, like they were back from the dead. In my imagination, their eyes look the same, the dummies' and the cats', flat and vacant as clay.

Dad wasn't talking about another school anymore. He was riding Win about finding a job. Marshall was a last resort. Win had lasted eight months, his longest stretch of school since he was sixteen, my age. The cadet core was made up of students in serious need of either discipline or toughening up, so it served as a sort of academic detour for wayward and weakling boys.

"The funny thing is nobody got better," my brother said. "The discipline problems just spent their down time kicking the shit out of the sissy kids."

He looked at me over the rim of a gurgling bong. He never once offered to get me high. I was the good kid in the family. It wasn't that I had no mischief in me, but my brother had blazed such a wide trail when it came to getting into trouble, that it was less effort to behave myself than to do something that would have surprised my parents into anger.

"Where'd you get the money for that stuff?" I pointed at his stash, a Ziploc sandwich bag, fat as a dictionary. My brother had no income that I knew about. He just slouched around the basement all day, skimming channels with the remote, looking for boxing on cable. Win was crazy for boxing.

"It doesn't cost much," he said, his voice pinched from holding smoke, his eyes crinkling at the corners. "You shouldn't ask so many questions, Jack. Questions can only lead to answers."

"What's that?" I said. "Pothead philosophy?"

He set the bong aside and came toward me in a boxer's crouch, swinging his torso from side to side, doing a loopy smile. I curled on the couch, folding my knees and ankles in tight to protect the vitals, covering my face with my forearms. He was only kidding around, but I knew from black-eyed experience that serious resistance could lead to trouble. It was better to lie still and take whatever abuse he had in mind. Red-bellies and Indian burns weren't so bad, compared to when my brother got out of hand.

He poked me in the ribs, tried to slap the underside of my balls with the back of his hand, but his heart wasn't in it. While he was trying to pry my arms apart, he kicked over the bong, spilling funky water on the carpet. That was just the sort of thing to set him off, and I tensed, waiting for things to get more painful, but they didn't. He said, "Motherfucker," and ground the wetness into the shag with his shoe, leaving a damp black footprint. He waved a can of Lysol around, jetting a phony pine scent into the room to cover the mildewy stink. It was a useless gesture. Dad was still so pissed at him, he wouldn't set foot in the basement if Win was there, unless it was to chew him out. And Mom, she didn't want to know what was going on. She closed her eyes to unpleasantness, like if she didn't see it, there couldn't possibly be anything wrong.

Win's girlfriend was Camille Crosby. Marshall had recently begun admitting women and Camille was one of only about six female cadets. She went AWOL on Friday nights. Win and I would drive the two hours to get her, me behind the wheel, because Dad didn't trust my brother with the car. He put me on assignment: Make sure Win stays out of trouble; short of that, keep me posted on whatever sort of mischief he's making for himself. Don't let me down, Jack. Win didn't mind not driving, because it meant he could have both hands free for the bong.

We'd wait around the corner from the guard gate, windows down to let the smoke trail out, until Camille emerged from the dark wall of pines. Sometimes we wouldn't hear her coming, and she would sneak up beside the car, draw a finger, warm as blood, along my throat, and tell me that I wouldn't last a minute in the bush. Camille was not the sort of girl I would have imagined for Win—she had biceps like a medium-sized guy and was planning on a career in the military—wasn't the sort of girl our parents would have liked, sweet and demure and well-mannered. She was pretty, I guess, in a plain way. No makeup, clear blue eyes and good skin. Brown hair, cut short and functional. As soon as she was in the car, she started kissing on my brother. They sat in the backseat and groped each other all the way back to town, misting the glass in their excitement. I had to run the defrost the whole time. When a car going the other direction lit our interior as it passed, I could see Win pushing her shirt up above her breasts, could catch flashes of her flat, milk-white stomach in the rearview mirror.

We'd grab a couple of six-packs and park in the woods on this old logging road near campus. There was an abandoned barn at the end of the road, which Win called their "pigsty of love," his voice, when he said the words, going cheap and gravelly. The barn was littered with stale hay. The roof sagged. The headlights danced through the open doors, like the beam of a movie projector.

We drank and bullshitted. They got stoned.

"You smoke?" Camille said to me.

"Don't answer that, Jack. Plead the fifth."

Win was hunched over the bong, this huge three-footer, like a prop from a reefer movie. Camille was lying on her stomach, chin in her hands. You could tell she felt bad about dragging me along, but I didn't mind. It beat rented movies and prank calls with my fat friend, Leo. I wasn't exactly what you would call popular.

She said, "You got a girlfriend?"

"Nope."

"He's playing the field," Win said, winking at me. "Jack's a lady-killer."

I fingered bark from a pine tree, getting sap under my nails. My hands, when I sipped my beer, smelled like turpentine. I wanted to think of something interesting to say. In a weird way, I was glad to have my brother back. The house was painfully quiet without him— my parents in front of the television every night, Mom reading a magazine glancing occasionally at the screen, Dad noodling around with work he brought home from the bank. I could hear ice in their martinis, loud as wind chimes, from all the way back in my room. At least the house was alive with Win in it. He was a strange current, passing through us, connecting us like a wire.

I said, "Did Win ever tell you about his amnesia?"

She shook her head and looked at him. He was blazing up again, sucking bubbles of smoke through the water. He waved his right hand, shaking pain from a scalded thumb. The little nest of marijuana glowed like a heated coil.

"He pretended for three days like he couldn't remember who we were," I said. "Like he couldn't remember anything. He walked around saying shit like 'This is sure a nice house you've got, ma'am.' Or 'Excuse me, sir, I just wanted to thank you for taking me in. I feel like I've been given a fresh start.' He was totally nonchalant."

"Oh my God." Camille smothered a laugh with her hand. "Tell me you're kidding?"

"No joke," I said.

Win raised his eyebrows. "I did that? I'm a funny guy."

"You're definitely something," she said. "I can't believe they bought it."

"Mom freaked," I said. "She took him to a neurologist. Made him look at old photo albums, played his favorite records, the works. Dad was a little skeptical, but Win stuck to his story."

"How'd they find you out?" she said to Win.

He kept smoking, so I told her the rest. How Win had found me kneeling by my bed, sheets gathered in my hands, praying that my big brother get his memory back. I was ten, Win fourteen. He knuckled my hair. He called me a dumbass, told me it was a scam. Neither of us heard my father at the door.

"Dad went totally psychotic," I said. "I thought he was going to kill us both."

We turned to Win, waiting for his take on things. He was holding the bong up to his eye, squinting down the tube, as if reading a fortune there. He looked up, did a double take, like he was surprised to find us watching him, and said, "*I'm* gonna go psychotic, if I can't get me some of that."

He pointed at her pants. This was what they came for. They slipped off to one of the rear stalls, far enough away that they thought I couldn't hear them. But I caught snatches of sound, Win lowing like a wounded cow and Camille's breathy whines. I sat on the roof of the car, waiting, waiting, the damp and gluey label of my beer bottle peeling away against my palm.

Win told Dad he had a job interview and caught a ride to town with me on my way to school. I don't know what he did all day, but he was waiting for me when class let out. The parking lot was full of students, boys taking off their ties, shouting to each other over the roofs of cars, girls lighting cigarettes, cranking radios. And there was Win, in the middle of all that blithe music, leaning against the passenger door of my hand-me-down Olds. I can't say I was glad to see him. He'd been wearing the same clothes every day for a week— a maroon sweatshirt, the hood cinched tight beneath his chin to hide his Afro, filthy camo pants, and Jesus sandals. Here, he was humiliating.

Win was trying to bum a cigarette from Heather Flynn. Heather was known around school for her tits and her nose, both fake. The nose, which had been sort of hawkish, was now arrow-straight with a catty upturn at the end. I'd liked her nose better before, but there was no arguing her chest improvement. This guy, a year older than me, blond with swimmer's shoulders, was leaning in her passenger window, arms crossed on the door. I was walking with Leo and ducked behind the trunk of a big oak. I didn't want to be seen with Win. At school, I didn't have a crazy brother. I told Leo to go on without me, there was something I had to do, and he was blank enough not to be suspicious, like all that extra padding on his head had made him a little dense. He shrugged and said, "See ya," and ambled on down to the lot, his eyes skimming like water bugs over my brother. I thought I'd wait until the crowd thinned out before going home.

My brother rapped on Heather's window, smiled, and made a smoking motion with his hand. She gave him a sneer, then went back to the boy. Win tapped the glass, still smiling, and waved. This time the window slid down, and I could see Heather's lips curling disdainfully around whatever she was saying. She closed the window in his face. The boy rolled his eyes. Win knocked again. I drew myself tight against the tree, pressed my cheek against the trunk until it hurt. I recognized the look on his face.

The boy stalked around the front of the car, Win talking the whole time. I couldn't hear what he was saying, but I could imagine his tone. I'd heard him talk like that to our father, his voice slick with malice. Win lowered his hood, his Afro bouncing into place like it was on springs. He gestured toward himself, took a step away from the car. People were watching now, a crowd beginning to gather, and the boy did an unsure look around, sizing up his audience. You could tell he was starting to realize that he'd gotten in over his head, but there was no backing out now. I could feel the bark biting my skin. The boy wound up and popped Win in the face, jacking him back a step, but that was it. He should have pressed his advantage—part of me wished he had—should have stayed on Win, kept hitting him, but he didn't and, after just a moment's hesitation, my brother finished the fight. He was crazy with violence, a hurricane burst of fists and knees and head butts. Win had a genius for hurting people. It was over so fast—Win looming over the boy, the boy curled fetally at his ankles—that no one had been able to help. And, now, after what they had just seen, they weren't about to get involved. I could see Leo gawking, Heather flattening her perfect nose against the glass. Win scanned the crowd—looking for me, I thought—then kissed his peace sign fingers and touched them to Heather's window.

One time, before military school, Win had snuck out on a school night, come home ugly drunk, and been confronted by our father. Dad asked him who he thought he was, drifting in so late, so tipsy— that's exactly what he said—worrying his mother half to death. Win thought "tipsy" was hilarious. He cocked his wrists, circled his fists, and did a little shuffle with his feet, Marquis of Queensbury style. He went from room to room breaking dishes, lamps, whatever he could find that would shatter, stopping now and then to shadowbox, his breath huffing through his nose, his fists clenched white, his arms working the air like pistons. He pitched an end table through a plate glass window, jagged shards littering the patio like falling stars. Win pumped his fists in the air, did a victory dance at the sight. He kept yelling this line from Muhammad Ali over and over. "I'm a bad man," he was shouting. "I'm so pretty."

Win was big enough that our father couldn't stop him physically, so Dad quit bellowing, stormed outside, found the axe, and hacked apart the dining room table, the wood splintering with a sickening sound like breaking bone. Win was shocked silent. I hid on the stairs and listened. I could hear my mother crying, her sobs making my stomach edgy, but I didn't think there was anything I could do for her. She said, "I'm calling Dr. Heller."

"You're not calling anybody," Dad said. "I've spent enough money for nothing to discredit every practicing shrink within a hundred miles of here. This isn't about our son wanting attention. This is about our son being an asshole. Look at Jack. When was the last time you saw Jack break a goddamn window."

I tensed at the sound of my name. Mom didn't answer. Dad said, "Jack, I know you're awake, boy. Come on down here. Right now."

I stayed where I was. I hated seeing my father like that, his features distorted, his breath coming in ragged gasps. And I couldn't bear to see my brother cowed. Dad called my name again, and this time I went slinking down the stairs. He said, "Jack, you ever broken a window? In your life, I'm talking about now. Tell the truth."

"No, sir."

I glanced at Win. I wanted him to understand that I didn't have a choice. He was squatting beside the wreckage, a broken table leg across his knees, watching us. The chandelier above the table swung side to side, throwing light around the room, like maybe Dad had caught it on a backswing. Win looked each of us over, one at a time, an odd smile on his lips, like we were strangers, surprising him with an impromptu dramatic performance.

"You're sure?" Dad said.

"Yes, sir."

"That's it, then," he said, raising his arms, the axe in one hand.

The next day, he did a careful accounting of the damages, excluding the dining room table, and made Win do hard labor around the yard, every day after school and every weekend from nine to five, working him for a dollar an hour, until he earned enough to make restitution. Win had no memory of the incident, but he did the work without complaint. After things had finally gotten quiet that night and my parents were in bed, he staggered back to my room and told me that our father was a good man. I would do myself a favor, he said, if I paid attention and didn't follow Win's example, He then proceeded to pass out on the floor beside my bed and wet his pants in his sleep.

I waited until Win had started home on foot before coming out from behind the tree. The parking lot cleared in a hurry. No one wanted to be around if an authority figure showed up asking questions. I found Win a mile or two from school and eased over to the curb so he could get in. When he saw me, he grinned, and I could see the broken edge of his front tooth like a tiny, crumbling tombstone.

"You get that tooth today?" I said.

"You saw the fight? Where the hell were you?" He dug around in the pocket of his sweatshirt and came out with a wrinkled joint. He pressed in the car lighter and waited, dangling the joint between his lips. "Naw, I got this yesterday. I can't believe you didn't notice before now. You're the watcher, man, you notice everything."

"Yesterday?"

"Yeah," he said. "Some Mexican guy. I wanted to see if he could take me, that's all. He turned out to be a serious disappointment."

I said, "You think that's a good idea? Fighting Mexicans?" I couldn't tell if he was serious.

"I'll fight anybody," he said.

"Of course you will," I said.

Right then, this dog—half Lab, half something else—came charging at the car, barking wildly, snapping at the tires, and I hit the brakes, slamming Win against the dashboard. The dog was obsessed with cars. He'd been run over half a dozen times and his durability was a sort of neighborhood legend. His bones, people said, regenerated like a lizard's tail. Win and I used to sit on the curb, wait for Dad to come home from work, and wager chores on whether or not the dog would get hit. Usually, I was ready for him, speeding by before he had a chance to build blitz momentum but today, I was distracted. I wanted to put some distance between me and my brother.

"Damn dog," Win said, getting himself straight in the seat. "I forgot about that fucker." He checked the joint for damage, saw that it was intact, and resituated it in the corner of his mouth. He hung himself out the window and shouted, "Go on, now. Beat it, dog. Don't make me get out of the car."

I crept along until the dog gave up, pretty houses sliding by in slow motion. I could feel the tires turning beneath us. Win said,

"That dog needs to get himself laid. One of these days his luck's going to run out. Pow, man." He smacked a forearm into his palm.

I turned right on Featherbed Road, our house at the end of the street. We grew up in this neighborhood and nothing much had changed. Same bricks, same people. I could see Mrs. Caldwell watering her lawn, silvery water arcing from the hose. In an hour or so, driveways would begin to fill with men returning from work, streetlamps would blink alive, one after another, gentling the twilight.

"You ever been with a girl?" he said.

I knew what he meant, and the answer was a resounding no. The closest I'd come to sex was a grudging spin-the-bottle kiss, which had been over before I could make my lips stop shaking. I wanted to conjure up a string of sexual exploits for him, to invent women of stunning beauty and refinement who'd given themselves up to me by the dozens, but I didn't. I sensed that he would know whether or not I was telling the truth. I shook my head.

"Yeah," he said. "It's a pain in the ass."

He was looking at his hands, turning them over, pale, fragile-looking palms to ragged knuckles. You would have thought he'd never seen them before, the way he was staring, or that he had, suddenly and without a single lesson, discovered them capable of playing the piano.

"What do you care?"

"You're my brother," he said. "I was thinking I could give you a hand." He paused, his words settling like ash. "You know, Camille might be convinced to help you out. She likes you, Jack."

My wrists thumped. I felt like I was being offered a bribe.

"I couldn't do that," I said. "She's your girlfriend."

"It would only be the one night. It wouldn't have to be charity or anything." The car lighter popped out and Win touched it to the tip of his joint, paper crackling backward. "You could fight me for her, if that's what you want." He gave me a smile, then, smoke curling over his lip, his tongue working rapturously over the place where the rest of his tooth had been.

* * *

That night, my father caught me masturbating. Camille called for Win and when I answered, she said, "Rescue me, baby. I'm going crazy all alone." I was in bed, supposedly reading my American history assignment, but really I was watching the ceiling fan turn above me, waiting for the mandatory two hours my parents had set aside for homework to be over. The textbook was in my lap and at the sound of her voice I felt an erection pressing up from beneath the book.

"Camille? It's me, Jack," I said. "I'll get Win."

"Oh hey, Jack," she said. "You've got your brother's voice. Wait a minute, listen to this."

I heard rustling, then nothing, and I imagined her holding the phone up so I could listen to the quiet. She said, "What'd you hear?"

"Nothing."

"Exactly," she said. "Put my man on the phone."

I yelled for Win and waited, listening to Camille's steady breathing, until he came on the line. I hung up, unzipped my pants and closed my eyes, working hard, trying to picture myself giving it to Camille, but something wasn't right. I kept seeing Win in my place, his chipped tooth gleaming in the light of my imagination. I'd forgotten to lock up and, right in the middle of things, the door swung open and there was my father, his mouth slack in surprise, the glare from my bedside lamp reflected on his glasses. I was stunned with humiliation. The hair on my neck quivered like insect legs.

He said, "Sorry, pal," and closed the door. I heard his loafers tapping down the stairs, then stop and, after a moment, I heard him coming back. I hustled my pants together and this time he rapped on the door and waited until I said, "What?" before coming in and taking a seat at the foot of the bed. He didn't look at me. He said, "I just wanted to make sure there wasn't anything we needed to talk about."

"Nope," I said. "I'm sixteen, Dad."

"I figured," he said.

My history book was beside us, still open to the page, and my father picked it up. He gave it a look and said, "Bastogne. Nuts." He chuckled to himself. I didn't have the slightest idea what he was talking about; I just wanted him gone. You would've thought that he'd already forgotten about catching me with my dick in my hand.

"Anything else, Dad?"

"As a matter of fact, there is something I'd like you to help me with." He tossed the book to the floor and pushed his fingertips beneath his glasses. He was still in his bank getup, his tie loosened, thrown back over his shoulder.

I said, "Right now?" but he ignored me.

"I was hoping you could tell me what's going on with your brother," he said, still not looking at me. He smoothed his tie between two fingers. "Your mother's worried sick over Win. She doesn't sleep at night." He paused, choosing his words carefully. "I feel like I owe someone an apology."

"Who, Dad?"

"I don't know," he said. "Somebody."

He rubbed his eyes again and, just for a second, I thought he was going to cry. I prayed silently that he wouldn't. I felt sorry for him, not knowing anything, not knowing what to do about his son. It was awful to see him like that. What he wanted, I thought, was to talk to me for a while, the good son. He wanted to be reassured that he hadn't made a complete hash of fatherhood, but I couldn't think of anything to say. I considered telling him what I knew, which wasn't much. Win had been fighting. I didn't know why. He was still smoking dope, but that would come as no surprise. The thing was, I couldn't figure out how it would help anybody for him to know. I could guess what would happen. There would be a blowup, serious shouting, and threats of violence with my mother's tears all mixed in. But, when it was over, we would all be just as unhappy.

"Sorry," I said. "I can't help you."

"That's too bad," he said, remotely. He patted me on the ankle and drifted down the hall, sort of dreamily, like he'd forgotten why he'd come. When he was gone, Win stuck his head in my room and said, "He asking about me?" I nodded, feeling like I was betraying a secret. He thumbed his chipped tooth and said, "Okay then."

When I was seven years old, Win convinced me that if I stripped naked, clutched my penis, and whispered, "Youbaby, youbaby, youbaby, you," over and over, I would become invisible. I wasn't a complete sucker, but I was a kid, and my brother had an answer for every question. I was already the pride of the family, reading and writing and monkeying around with simple division, things that would make any mother proud. And Win was already Win. When my parents' friends came over to visit, they asked about me first. It came as quite a shock to my mother and the bridge ladies, when I cruised into the room without a stitch on, my little kid balls tight with apprehension, chanting my perverted mantra. They scattered cards, kept the table between me and them. My mother was flattened. Her eyes glazed over, and her face went pale. She didn't say a word.

I found Win in the backyard—he'd been watching through the window—lying in the grass, crippled with laughter. I wasn't mad at him. I just couldn't figure out what had gone wrong. How had they been able to see me? Win got himself together, made me sit beside him and explained that he had only been kidding. There was no way to turn yourself invisible. I was more disappointed than anything else. The yard had been recently cut and grass clippings were caught in his hair and stuck to his shirt where he'd been rolling around, laughing at me. I was glad to make him laugh.

"You're right," Win said. "It'd be nice if nobody could see you."

I plucked the clippings from his hair and shoulders. I said, "Yeah."

"That's the trouble," he said. "They can."

It was Leo who told me Win was dealing. Sweet, fat, guileless Leo sat beside me in the cafeteria, where I was working on a ham and cheese sandwich, and said, "I saw your brother down in the parking lot selling marijuana this morning. I think that's what he was doing.

I thought that only happened at public school, but I saw him. Hey, are you coming over tomorrow night?" He touched the lenses of his glasses with two greasy fingertips, smudging them. Leo didn't care that Win was my brother, and I didn't think he was intending to do anything with his information, both of which I was grateful for. Leo had been unliked and unnoticed for so long, he'd gotten used to being ineffectual. The world went gladly on without him. Sometimes, I hated being his friend. He had given up, resigned himself to being unnecessary. I felt implicated by his complacency. But at that moment, the cafeteria ablaze with voices, Leo telling me, "There's good movies on cable tomorrow," if I'd been called upon to choose between him and my brother, I would have taken Leo in a heartbeat.

I let Leo have my sandwich and hurried down to the lot, but Win was already gone. I stood there a minute, among the somnolent cars, my heart flopping, feeling like I wanted something to happen. It wasn't that Win was selling pot; he could do whatever he wanted, for all I cared, as long as he didn't do it in my life. I had enough trouble getting along without him. I piled in the car and headed home, hauling ass through the neighborhood. The dog made a rush at me, his body low and hard, but I was too fast for him to catch. I lurched through the front door, stormed back to Win's room, and found him kneeling on the bathroom floor, nursing his swollen hands in a toilet full of ice. At the sight of him like that, his mouth tight, his eyes wide and innocent with pain, all the anger I had been feeling evaporated.

He said, "They hurt too much to turn on the faucet."

He showed me his hands, cradled them on his belly like broken-winged birds. His knuckles were cracked and bloody, the bones shattered, his fingers dappled with bruise colors, as flaccid and puffy as wet bread. There was a crust of blood rimming his nostrils, a runny scab at his hairline, and a bluing lump on his right cheekbone. We were alone, Dad still at work, Mom out running errands or something. The house was quiet.

"Dad's gonna shit himself," I said.

"Too late to worry about that," he said, his voice thick, like his tongue was swollen. He did a wincing grin. The phone was ringing in another room.

"I don't even wanna know what happened," I said. "I don't wanna have any secrets to keep. I'm gonna get in enough trouble for leaving school."

"Afraid the old man'll get it out of you?" Win said. "He's a pro, that's for sure. I'm surprised he doesn't have a chair in the basement with a bare bulb dangling over it. For interrogations, get it?"

"We've got to get you out of here," I said.

He shook his head. "Nothing we can do."

"They can't see you like this, Win," I said. "Not so soon. It'd kill 'em."

I gripped his elbow and helped him off the floor. He wobbled a little on his feet, righted himself, then yanked his arm free. Win wouldn't let me take him to the emergency room so I just got him to the car and started driving. I was thinking about when my father brought him home from Marshall, both of them emerging from the car, slump-shouldered and bewildered like smashup survivors. How hushed and sad that ride must have been. Out of nowhere, Win said, "Camille hates Muhammad Ali." His voice was strange, too timid and small for his body all of a sudden. "She thinks he converted to Islam to keep himself out of Vietnam. And, if you knew Camille, you'd know that was an unforgivable offense in her eyes." He settled his head back against the seat and closed his eyes. He looked so unfamiliar to me that, just for a moment, I couldn't remember his name.

I drove him up to Marshall, stopping on the way to let Camille know we were coming, and the three of us stashed ourselves away at the barn. He had his head in Camille's lap, was holding his hands up to see them better. They looked diseased in the gray evening light. He had taken a couple of bong hits, wedging the tube between his wrists, while Camille worked the lighter, and was feeling easy. He kept saying, "You should see the other guys." Camille was stroking his head, her fingers snagging in his hair. She was still wearing her cadet uniform—pine nettle green slacks, a soup-brown tunic with her rank pinned into the collar, and blocky black shoes, polished to a reflective shine. I couldn't stop myself from pacing.

"What are we gonna do?"

"I don't know," Camille said. "The hospital is still a good idea."

"Bad idea," Win said. "I'm fine, okay. You should—"

"I don't want to hear about it, Win," I said. "I don't care what you did."

"Jack's in charge," he said.

He tilted his head back to look at Camille. She smiled at him and covered his eyes with her hand. It was still a few hours from dark, but the moon was up, a flat white disc nestled among the branches of the trees. I said, "We can't just leave him like this. We have to do something."

"What do you have in mind?" Camille said.

"I don't know."

"I know," Win said. "You two have sex. I'll watch."

Camille slapped his chest hard, and he grunted. I said, "It's okay, Win. The party's over. You can quit being an asshole now."

"Seriously," he said. "I told you I'd ask her. Hey, Camille, how would you feel about having sex with my little brother? It's okay with me, if it's okay with you."

"Stop it, Win," she said, getting to her feet, dumping Win's head from her lap.

"He's a virgin," Win said.

I couldn't look at her. I was thinking that somehow she knew about the other night; she could see it in the blood hurrying to my temples, knew that she was in my thoughts, when my father caught me. I remembered Leo, what he'd told me, and I was angry again, my throat and shoulders tight.

Camille said, "Win, don't make trouble. You've done enough."

"I promised Jack," he said. "I told him I would help him."

"I don't need your help. *You* need help," I said.

"C'mon, Jack. Who's kidding who?"

He drew himself up, slowly, painfully.

"Win, stop," Camille said. "He's your brother."

"A genetic fluke," Win said. "Look at him. He's pathetic."

That's when I hit him. It wasn't much, a reflex. He took a step toward me, and I rapped him in the mouth, snapping his head back. For this one terrifying instant, the world went quiet, and it wasn't so much like silence rushing in, as all the sound sucking out, like an undertow. He just looked at me, smiling, blood running in the spaces between his teeth. His arms were at his sides, palms turned out, his chin raised just slightly, sallow light playing on his face and hands. This is where my memory goes funny on me. I know that something came loose in me. I remember the feeling, like shrugging away old skin. I know that I hit him again, harder, wanting to hurt him, and I kept hitting him, over and over. And I know that he didn't resist. He couldn't resist. His hands were useless. But in my memory, Win is talking as I hit him, saying "That's it," and, softly, "Yes," and, "There." He keeps standing for a long time, staggering, dropping to his knees, but always regaining his feet. Camille tries to pull me away, but I shake her loose and beat my brother back down. I can feel the bone and cartilage in his nose coming apart beneath my fist, the pulpy lids of his eyes. In my uncertain memory, he keeps whispering, and I keep hitting him, my hands burning, until he runs out of things to say.

My father met us at the emergency room. When he came in, Camille and I were sitting in the waiting room, drinking coffee. I had called him at work, so Mom didn't know yet. I hadn't told him any details on the phone, just that Win was hurt. He stopped a few feet away, asked me where they were keeping him. I stood and pointed, and he stalked off down the hall. A black woman was sitting across from us, her hair done in cornrows, and I watched her cheating at solitaire. Whenever she got into trouble, she'd just peek under the stacks on the table, find the card she needed, and slip it into the deck, real sneaky, like she was fooling herself.

When my father came back, he said, "Jesus. What happened? His face is all bandages." He took the coffee from me, our knuckles brushing, and I could see his hands trembling. "Where's the doctor? I want to talk to the doctor."

"The doctor is hiding," the woman said, looking at us, the beads in her hair ticking. "He's dodging work, like everybody else."

"Thank you," my father said. Then to me, "What happened, Jack?"

I said, "I did it."

I wasn't feeling sorry yet, though I knew that would come. I wasn't feeling anything. I wanted to get whatever it was that I had coming.

"Did what?"

"I did this to Win."

The woman said, "Oh, Lord." My father shot her a glance, then turned his eyes to me. I knew that look. His squeeze the truth out of you look, eyes narrow, gaze hard. He said, "Jack, now is not the time for fucking around. Your brother is on a roller cot, behind a shitty little paper curtain, and it's important that I know what happened."

"I told you what happened."

He turned to Camille, looked her up and down, registering the uniform, and said to her, "Is that right?"

She nodded, cautiously. We hadn't spoken since the car. My father looked into the coffee cup, wisps of steam rising from the surface. He shook his head, took a sip, and shook his head again, grimacing the coffee down. For the second time in a week, I thought he was going to cry. But he didn't. He said, "Why?"

After a while, I said, "I don't really know."

He nodded, eyes still on the cup, like that was the most reasonable thing he'd heard in a long time. A group of paramedics came banging through the double doors, then, pushing a man on a gurney, voices loud and hurried, skidding down the corridor and out of sight. All of us, except my father, rubbernecked their passing. He didn't acknowledge them, just sat there, still nodding, mesmerized. All of a sudden, like he was just then realizing what was in his hands, he said, "When did you start drinking coffee?"

Win is, as the saying goes, in the army now. He did his basic at Fort Dix, New Jersey, then shipped down to Fort Knox, Kentucky, home of the gold depository, for tank training. He says he wants to drive a tank. It's been eleven months, and we still haven't talked about what happened. Except for me to say, "I'm sorry." And him to say, "Don't worry." I explained to him that I took the blame for all his injuries. There was no need for our parents to know about anything that had happened before. So I still don't know how he came to be in the bathroom, numbing his hands in the john. A drug deal gone bad, I tell myself, whenever I start wondering, though probably that isn't true. I won't ask. He'll tell me if he wants to. It's not important.

When we brought my brother home from the hospital, Mom and Dad were so concerned with ministering to him, they forgot about what I'd done for a while. I hid in the basement, listening to their steps shuffling above me, back and forth from the kitchen and the medicine cabinet to Win's room, and the whole thing began to seem like something that I had seen on television. The details fuzzed over. Like Win talking while I hit him. It might be that it just happened that way in my memory. It might not be true at all.

By the time my parents remembered me, most of the sting had gone out of them. Dad made an effort at anger, puffing himself up and doing some shouting, like he knew how he was supposed to feel but couldn't quite get it right, and Mom nodded and said, "He's right," and she cried a little for me. It was strangely pleasant, sitting there with them, answering their questions as best I could, each of us knowing our part in the discussion, even though mine was new. They were my parents, and I was their son and that was enough.

We write to each other, Win and I. He still hears from Camille, too; she's going to join up as soon as she graduates. I got a letter from him the other day. He said he had gotten in a little trouble with his CO and had been busted down to janitorial detail. Not to worry, though, because part of his job was pushing a broom in the depository and he thought that was okay. He was usually alone, not counting sentries, and it was always dead quiet, except for the shushing of the broom on the concrete. The vault was "environmentally maintained," he said, which in army terms means "cold as a witch's titty." The ceiling was sky-high and the gold—"Oh, man, you should see it"—millions of gold bricks stacked in neat rows, as far as the eye can see. He wrote, "I'd like to be driving my tank by now, but how can I complain when all the guys are out humping, and I've got AC." In my imagination, I see him gliding his push broom, his image reflected over and over on the gold bars, like the walls of some crazy sultan's palace. He has five o'clock shadow on his shaved head. He's whistling a song that has been nagging him pleasantly all day. He notices his reflection in the gold and stops, unable for a second to recognize himself, like, all of a sudden, he has amnesia, like he's seeing the world again for the very first time.

The Man Who Went Out
for Cigarettes

I came home from work one night and found my wife sitting in her
wheelchair beside the bed. She was wearing a midnight-blue
bustier with matching garters, the lace tops of her stockings just
showing above the blanket on her lap. Marilyn, my wife. She'd spent
some time on her hair. It was brushed smooth, lay on her shoulders
coppery and fine, the ends curled. Her fingers worked the blanket,
her legs ghostly beneath it, like covered furniture. She didn't say a
word. While she watched, I scattered change on the dresser, took
off my tennis shoes and wet socks. I worked as a deck hand on a
sportfishing charter, and my T-shirt and shorts were smeared with the
evidence of my labor, slick scales, like sequins, and fish-gut hand-
prints. Naked, I carried the whole reeking mess down to the laundry
room and dropped it in the machine. I'd redone the halls in black
rubber tracks so she could get around easier. The house was quiet.

Nothing had changed when I returned.

I sat on the edge of the bed and said, "I stink."

"Not too bad," she said.

She touched my thigh. I said, "What do you want me to do?"

"Pick me up, Duncan," she said. "Put me on the bed."

I'm accustomed to it, now, carrying her to bed, cradling her slender, indifferent legs, like sleeping children. I can move enough for

both of us. But that night, I dropped her onto the mattress, clumsy as a drunk. Tugged at her knees and ankles like they were pillowcases full of stones. Relax, she said, slow down, be gentle. I couldn't stop apologizing. To compensate for her stillness, Marilyn ran her hands along the backs of my arms, dragged her fingernails up and down my spine. She moaned and carried on. I couldn't stop thinking that I was hurting her—she was so brittle and small—imagining that her hips would give out beneath us, and I'd have to rush her to the hospital, all the emergency personnel thinking how I was making love to a crippled woman.

"Are you all right?" I said. "Is everything okay?"

"I'm fine," she said. "You don't have to stop."

She put her hands on my backside and pushed me into her. My skin was going clammy. I looked over my shoulder at her legs, splayed beside mine, her feet cocked outwards. I could feel myself slackening inside her.

"Can you even feel me?" I said.

"Yes," she said. "I can feel you."

I blushed at her lie, pressed my face into her neck.

"You can't, can you."

She paused, then said, "Not the way I used to. But I can feel you. I promise."

My bones felt watery. I kept waiting for her to get angry, to tell me how useless I was and that I wasn't even good for sex anymore. She was my wife. I wanted her to get angry. Like at the hospital, right after it happened. Her face was all matted hair and blood, her cheeks pressed together by this device they used to stabilize her head. I leaned over the gurney so she could see me, and she said, "Someone's sitting on my legs. Tell this fat sonofabitch to get off my legs."

I didn't know what else to do. Her eyes were nothing but heat. I looked at a spot in the air where a face would have been.

"Get the fuck off my wife's legs," I said.

Now, my eyes were closed tight. Marilyn kept trailing her fingernails along my spine. She smelled powdery and a little stale, the way a baby smells. The lace on her bustier was like scales against my chest.

After a while, she said, "Would it help if we turned out the light?"

I rolled off of her and put my feet on the floor, the room pitching under me the way you can still feel the ocean in your legs when you've just set foot on dry land. I didn't know what was wrong with me. She was my wife of seven years. I lit a cigarette, tapped the ashes into my tennis shoe.

"Duncan?" she said.

"No," I said. "You're beautiful. I told you."

"You didn't say that," she said. "You haven't looked at me in three hundred and seventeen days."

"Well," I said. I rubbed my eye with the heel of my hand. "Listen, Marilyn, I need to get out for a while. I need to get some cigarettes, okay."

Marilyn was small enough that I could barely sense her presence on the bed behind me. She had a way of going so quiet and still you didn't even know she was there. Like after I brought her home from the hospital and she had given up on anger. She'd have me roll her over to the window before I left for work, except instead of facing the ocean, she wanted her chair aimed at the wall, so the water was on her left. When I asked her why, she said, "I want to see the world sideways. It'll be like the window of a car."

At first, I thought this was about the accident. She was trying to re-create, in some bleak and dangerous manner, the view she had when she was sideswiped. But I came to believe that it was something else entirely, though I didn't know exactly what, the way she just sat there without making a sound, the tides always rising and falling on her left, the sun beating down on the road between our house and the beach, the wind catching sand from the dunes. When we ate dinner, she sat sideways at the table. When we slept, she lay on her left side, facing me, her eyes on my back. It was about this time that I started working more overnight trips. Shark fishing. I couldn't sleep at home, and on the boat, I didn't have to sleep at all. We'd drift, quietly, chumming the surface with butcher's leavings and fish entrails, calling the sharks up from deeper water. Me and Meadowlark, the other mate, this little Bahamian guy with a seventies Afro, sitting on deck, stealing beers from the coolers of the paying customers.

It was also about this time that I cheated on my wife. Two couples had come on board the day before, excited and doing jokes about catching a great white in the Gulf of Mexico. When I told one of the women, Gail, that there were no great whites in the Gulf, just makos and hammerheads and blacktips and so on and we'd be lucky if we caught a shark at all, she gave me this big smile and said, "You're so literal. I love that about you."

That night she appeared on deck wearing nothing but a T-shirt and panties. Everyone else was sleeping down below. We were supposed to wake them at midnight. She brought a joint and the three of us passed it around. After a while, she left us, slipped along the gunnel to the bow, her legs bright as ice in the moonlight. Meadowlark said, "She want to fuck you, mon."

"You're crazy," I said.

I looked toward the bow, but I couldn't see her anymore. She must have been lying against the wheelhouse. I couldn't see anything except ocean.

"I'm not crazy." Meadowlark stood and pissed off the side of the boat. When he was finished, he turned toward me, his dick in his hand and said, "You see dis?" He waved his penis at me. "You see how healthy she is? How black and strong?"

"Very impressive," I said.

"Daht's cause I fucking all the time. Your wife in de chair," he said. "You got to use it, mon. She like to fall right off."

So I went forward, found Gail, and made hurried love to her, her husband asleep below the deck, my wife at home with useless legs, the deepest water aswarm with hungry sharks. When I got home, I thought about telling Marilyn what had happened, but decided against it. I told myself that she didn't need to hear something like that. Things were hard enough already.

Marilyn and I live on the only inhabited island off the coast of Alabama. There's a legend about the place dating from when the French had just settled Mobile. It seems that some wise frog had the bright idea to use Dauphin Island to keep pigs for the colony. No need for fences, because everyone knew that pigs couldn't swim. Just strand a couple of swineherds out here, ship them food and water. Only they were wrong about the pigs. The story goes that one night the swineherds woke to this preposterous racket, branches snapping, water splashing like someone was dropping boulders into it, and they found the pigs making a break for the mainland. The sound between the island and the Gulf was full of squealing pigs, hundreds of them, paddling like hell with their hard little hooves for the freedom of the shore.

Sometimes, as we're cruising out of the marina, taking the slow curve in the channel between Dauphin Island and Petite Bois— pronounced "petty boy" in Alabama—I imagine those pigs in the water, snouts pointed snobbishly skyward, coarse hair slick with salt water, and I can't help but laugh. One of the paying customers will ask me what's so funny, and I'll tell the story, and all at once, I own the ocean and the white beach and the bend in the shore where the pigs reached land. I'm part of all of this and all of this is part of me.

I tried to explain the feeling to Marilyn once. This was before we were married. We were sitting on the porch looking out over the marsh grass behind my house, moths tapping against the screen. She was still in her uniform—Marilyn worked at the Dauphin Island Bird Sanctuary before the accident, and she had this ranger costume, safari shirt, brown shorts rolled at the cuff, her hair tucked into a cap, hiking boots. I used to tell her she looked like a boy scout—her legs stocky and solid-looking in the porch shadows. She asked me why I was still doing the work that college kids did on their summer vacations. She didn't say it mean; she just wanted to know. I told her the story about the pigs, and when I was finished she lifted my hand to her lips and kissed my knuckles, like that was the sweetest thing she'd heard in a long time. She wrinkled her nose at the way I smelled. "Let's get you cleaned up," she said and led me by the hand to the tub where she proceeded to wash me until I was absolutely pristine, scrubbing my fingernails, the insides of my thighs, my pale and water-logged feet. You could have eaten off my belly. Marilyn did kiss me there, when we were through. And on my pink knees and my chest and at my widow's peak. It was nothing like bathing her af-ter the accident with all her floundering and tears and her rubbery mannequin legs. I gleamed beneath her lips. I can't remember feeling so clean before, or since.

That's what I was thinking after I failed to make love to my wife.

I was sitting in the bed of the truck—my old Ford rigged with a wheelchair lift—the beach a flat white strip across the road. The ocean was nothing dark. Even as I brought my third cigarette in a row up for a drag, I could smell the dead fish on my fingertips. We'd had a crew out for bottom fishing today. All afternoon, I sliced bait minnows for paying customers, fixed the silvery squares on half-inch hooks, removed gasping snapper and graying triggerfish, as vivid as a painter's palette when still beneath the water, and dropped them into the live well, where they flitted around in a holding pattern until the customer, who had paid handsomely for the privilege, was ready for them to die.

Now, I sniffed my hands, blew smoke across my knuckles. Sand danced on the pavement. The air was humid enough it was like breathing through water. My heart flopped in my chest. I started thinking what it would be like to just crank up the car and go, how it would feel to be one of those guys that you hear about who says, "Honey, I'm going out for a pack of smokes," and closes the door behind him and keeps driving until he has another life. He hangs a left in front of the house, like he does every other day, and suddenly he's in Texas with a new wife and a couple of kids and his own boat and there's boundless green water everywhere he looks. The wind is full of pirate voices and those kids are going crazy because their daddy has a marlin at the end of his line, and his wife is like something from a magazine, all tan and blonde and filled up with love. He learns to play tennis with his daughter and teaches his son the proper way to fillet an amberjack. He makes love to his wife. At night, when the kids have grown and gone away, the two of them sit on the porch and watch the water. And he never thinks about his old life, never once looks in the rearview mirror when he's driving to visit his wife's grave up on the flowered hillside and thinks about what he left behind, the other woman and their past together. He has made a clean break, the man who went out for cigarettes, and he knows that if he lets himself remember, even for a second, it will be as if not a single year has passed, and he will be jerked backward through space and time and find himself sitting in the bed of a truck, smelling the stink of his hands, and wishing that he were the sort of man who could leave his wife.

I flicked my cigarette into the road, sparks scattering like bees, and hopped down from the truck. I watched the galaxies moving in the sky. Our bedroom window made a yellow square against the darkness. Beyond the window was my wife. Inside, I stopped by the laundry room, poured detergent in with my work clothes, got the machine going, then fixed a glass of beer in the kitchen and carried it back toward Marilyn. The runners made everything real quiet, and the only light was at the end of the hall. I had a strange feeling, then, woozy and disoriented, like I was surfacing in deep water, moving through all the years of my life with Marilyn, all the times I kissed her appendix scar, all the nights we spent talking about the children we would have together, all the days on wintry beaches after the tourists had gone home for the season, all of those things piled one on top of the other to arrive at this moment. Marilyn was still in bed. She opened her eyes when I came in, but I could tell she hadn't been asleep.

"I never heard the car start," she said.

"Listen," I said, taking a seat on the edge of the bed. "You remember those swimming pigs?"

"That's not what I expected you to say," she said. I could see her reflection in the window. She was looking at my back. After a moment, she said, "Okay. What about them?"

"The woods upstate are crawling with wild pigs," I said. "The kin of those jailbreak pigs. You can hunt them all year long, there's so many of them."

"So?" she said. "The woods are full of sausage. So?"

"I just wonder sometimes how they knew which way to swim. I mean no one even thought they could swim in the first place. How'd they know not to take off into the Gulf and drown?"

Marilyn didn't answer. She propped up on her elbows and inched back until she was leaning against the headboard. I could hear her breathing, and it seemed to me that I could almost make out her thoughts. She wanted to ask me what the hell I was talking about at a time like that. Those pigs, she wanted to say, didn't have anything to do with us. And she would have been right, if she'd said it, they didn't. It was just something that popped into my head when I should have been thinking about my wife. But she didn't say anything. I started to light another cigarette, but I didn't really want it, so I just held the thing, tapped the filter against my thumbnail. Finally, Marilyn spoke. She said, "Look at me."

"I keep waiting for this to get easier, Marilyn."

"Look at me," she said again.

I didn't turn around right away. Nothing had happened yet, and I wanted to hold on to the feeling I had just then. The air was full of choices, and it was only a matter of time before I picked the one that I could live with.

Sundays

Sundays it seems as if my neighborhood is populated entirely by single mothers. Gin Parker, who lives diagonally across from me, is the oldest, maybe thirty-five, and then Ashlynn Wolfe with a braid in her hair to her waist that she swears has not been cut in sixteen years. I am only eight months to the neighborhood and don't know whether or not I believe her. The Widow Friar—she lost her husband in the Gulf War—is the only non-divorceé, except of course Rachel, lovely Rachel. She told the father of her daughter, Macy, to stand clear. She had him sign papers. All of us live on the dead end of Cottonstocking Lane in fixer-uppers, the realtor called them, small older homes with wood floors and chipped paint, loaded with "personality." A gigantic oak tree spreads its branches all the way across the street, filtering the light, casting intricate shadows.

I am standing in my own yard, barefoot, pressing my toes into the grass, smoking a cigarette. It is warm for February. In the spring and summer, I will push a lawn mower for them or cut back overgrown hedges, but mostly I just watch them, watch their children flashing back and forth and shout to them across the street. There are cutoff shorts today, seeing the light for the first time in months, and white knees. Sometimes there are cookies. What I like most of all is to wake up late on Sunday and lie in bed and listen to them a while before getting up and going outside. Their voices, like rain on windows, masks the silence that is in my house. But it never rains on Sundays.

"It's almost noon, Wiley," Gin says. "You lazy white boy."

She sends a Frisbee wobbling across the street into my yard, and her son, Paul, chases after it without looking for cars. For the first few months, my heart stopped when I saw something like that, one of the children breaking alone into the street, but I relaxed over time. No one ever drives to our dead end.

Gin catches Paul before he can reach the Frisbee and lifts him, cocks her hip, and sits him there. She is pretty, going ever so slightly to fat but in a good way, in the way that her son is still soft and fleshy. She and Paul have the same wheat blond hair.

"Great day," I say, blowing smoke. "I almost feel like exercising."

She laughs and lets Paul down and he runs over to collect the Frisbee, orange with Day-Glo lime letters that say "R U SERIOUS."

"You need a haircut," she says.

"You think?" I say, pushing my hair back from my forehead, where it is too long, and letting it fall over my eyes. "I thought I had a sort of Hollywood thing going."

"Yeah, that's right," she says. "You and Johnny Depp all the way to the bank."

I flex my fingers at Paul, making what I think is a catching motion, and he winds up and throws, missing me wildly. The Frisbee lands on its side and goes rolling back across the street. Ashlynn sends one of her twin girls to bring it back and the twin—I can never tell them apart—meets Paul in the street and hands it over, shyly, as if passing him a love letter. Both of them are embarrassed.

Gin says, "Come by tomorrow about six and I'll neaten it up for you."

"You're the boss," I say.

It is a quiet morning. Voices matching the thin winter sunlight. Widow Friar has not come out yet with her boisterous daughter

Tammy, the oldest of the children on Cottonstocking. A light breeze pushes leaves and makes my smoke dance.

"You're coming tonight, right?" Gin says. She already knows the answer.

Every Sunday night one of us hosts a potluck. I work the barbecue, pretending I don't speak the language of the kitchen, hamming up my clumsiness there for the benefit of my neighbors. For my birthday, they gave me a "Kiss the Cook" apron and we wound up red-wine drunk, me with perfect lip-shaped kisses on my cheeks and neck and forehead. They stopped between each kiss to reapply plum-colored lipstick so it would show.

Rachel and Macy are coming up the sidewalk toward us and Macy is talking rapidly, moving her hands for emphasis, twisting one around the other, as if casting a spell. She can't be more than three feet tall, twelve inches for each year of her life. I am constantly surprised that something that small can, well, can think. I wonder how her eyes see the world. I found a battered quarter in the street the other day and gave it to her, and she told me that she loved me. Just like that.

Her mother is taller than most men, maybe six-two, with boyishly short hair and real shoulders. Length is her crowning feature, reedy legs and long, slender arms. Narrow wrists. These combine to make her motion a sort of wonderful, mesmerizing slink. Rachel teaches geometry at the same parochial high school where I am a teacher of Latin and Greek. I often see her in the hall, passing the little window in my classroom door, mostly just her chin and slim neck because of her height.

My students repeat after me, *"Amo, amas, amat, amamus, amatis, amant."*

Sometimes, Richard Davies, the school guidance counselor, and I will sit on the iron benches in the school courtyard and watch Rachel in her classroom, squirrels perched on her windowsill eating acorns. I like Richard because he doesn't care enough about his job to worry about losing it. I once overheard him tell fretful parents, "Your daughter has some serious fucking problems."

I watch Rachel, watch her moving back and forth in front of the blackboard, stretching on tiptoe to pull down the screen for the overhead projector or using a yardstick to draw perfect equilateral triangles. Her face lighting in response to something a student has said. Richard elbows me and says, "How would you like to get her in the bag?" or "Imagine those legs around your back." And I want to tell him that I have had her in my arms, that I have kissed those shoulders. I don't tell him, because in the end nothing happened, not really.

I had walked Rachel home from one of Widow Friar's potlucks, and we had been drinking. As we were saying good night in front of her house, all of the lights on the street went out simultaneously, windows going black, streetlights blinking off, soaking us in darkness. We discovered later that a branch had fallen across one of the transformer lines, shutting down our whole area, but at the time it seemed ominous and frightening and full of strange magic, both of us jumping and putting our arms around each other. We laughed but didn't let go right away. She invited me in and we talked for a long time and we kissed a different kiss from my birthday. But I heard her daughter down the hall, heard Macy or maybe I just thought I did, heard her call to her mother through her sleep. I couldn't go any farther.

Now, Rachel crouches next to her daughter and both of them look at the sky. She has an arm around Macy's back and they are talking, softly. She turns to Gin and me and says, "What do y'all think those clouds look like? We think seahorses."

The clouds are low and compact, each one separate and identifiable, white, like clouds at the beach. They aren't bruised thunderheads, but away from the ocean and the sand, they are somehow threatening. They look painted on.

"What about ships?" I say. "The Aegean fleet sailing to Troy for Helen's love."

Rachel and Macy frown. Gin kicks me, playfully, in the ankle and says, "You know, I always thought Latin teachers were jackasses but I had high hopes for you."

Rachel covers her daughter's ears and Macy puts her hands on top of her mother's. She doesn't try to pry Rachel's hands away, just curves her fingers around them, content with her mother's hands softly on her face, wind, I imagine, from the cup of palms, rushing in her ears like the roar of ocean in a seashell.

"Watch your fucking mouth," Rachel says. She winks at me.

I cross the street to them, extending my hand to Macy.

"Hello, Madame, may I have this dance," I say in an exaggerated French accent, kneeling, making myself her height, arranging my arms as if I am already holding her.

"No," she says, pressing herself against her mother, but when I make a heartbroken face, pulling my lips down, squinting as if I might cry, she adds, "I can do a summerso," and brightens in apology. She has already learned the effect of batting her eyelashes.

"A somersault," Rachel says, clarifying. "Show the crazy man what you can do, baby."

Macy steps into the grass, bends, lowering her head to the ground, balancing with her hands, her dress falling up around her shoulders, and falls to one side. We all applaud and Macy just lies on the damp grass, one arm flung over her eyes dramatically as if her performance has left her spent. Her smile is creeping out from beneath that soft forearm.

A door slams behind us. We turn and see Widow Friar coming out, leading a man, shyly, by the hand. He is rawboned and crew cut. All of the women begin hooting and catcalling, and the man just stands by the Widow's car, embarrassed but happy, waiting for her to unlock the passenger door, rubbing the top of his head. Those are not bad shoes to be in, all of that attention lavished on you. For an instant, I am envious.

Driving past us, Widow Friar leans out of the window and says, "I always had a thing for soldiers."

"You whore," yells Gin and right at that moment, the wind swirls up, whipping through the big oak, making the branches cast off wild shadows and streaks of light, as if the tree and the street itself were laughing with us.

I am standing in front of the full-length mirror on the back of my bathroom door, getting ready for the party. I am naked and my hair is still wet, slicked back. In the reflection, I can see six steaks on three Styrofoam trays sitting on the back of the toilet, bleeding watery blood. I am, as usual, bringing the grill fare but I didn't take the steaks out of the freezer soon enough and thought that maybe in the heat and steam of the shower they would thaw faster in here. My khakis and shirt are hanging on the towel rack behind me. I can see a green dry-cleaning tag still pinned into the collar but I decide to leave it in. I will let one of the ladies discover it and take it out for me. I will let them think I can't take care of myself.

I sometimes think that I'm not much of a teacher, that I worry too much that the students won't think I'm suitably impressive. That I spend too much time looking at the pretty young girls, the girls that have to be reminded to button their blouses higher up, wondering if they find me attractive.

I tell my students stories to make the dry words more lively. If I had a time machine, I say, and could only use it once, I would slip back to Thebes, as quick and invisible as thought, at the exact moment that Croesus asked Solon to tell him the name of the happiest man in the world. Croesus expected the answer to be himself, but it wasn't. Solon said that the happiest man was an Athenian who had married young, seen the healthy births of his children and his children's children, and had died honorably, his heart empty of regret, in defense of his home. I can picture Croesus, brow knitted with derision. How can a dead man be happier than a king? Who is the second happiest then? The second happiest men, Solon told him, were two brothers who yoked themselves to an oxcart and pulled their mother five miles over rough country to a religious festival, because the oxen hadn't been brought in from the fields soon enough. In her gratitude, their mother prayed that the gods grant her sons the greatest blessing that men can have. And her prayer was answered, the gods causing the brothers to fall into a peaceful sleep, the deepest sleep, and never woke again. I would like very much to see the look on Croesus's face, there in his throne room, dusty sunlight slanting in. I can imagine it, his mouth and eyes going slack, see it as if he were in the classroom with me, proud smile, fading to bewilderment, then finally, as Solon's meaning creeps over him, to terror.

I finish dressing and go outside, down the steps, watching my feet in the dark. Halfway across the street, I'm nearly run down by Tammy, the Widow's daughter, on her bicycle. She flashes by in front of me, a blur, all motion, and skids to a stop at the dead end, kicking up gravel. Though it is the wrong time of year, there are fireflies swirling in the bushes behind her. Tammy is eleven years old, maybe twelve. She rides by again, this time behind, close enough that I can feel the wind in her wake, then circles me once, like a motorcycle gang, before standing in the pedals and biking up the street the other way.

"Shouldn't you be at Rachel's?" I say. Tammy baby-sits for Rachel on Sunday nights.

Without looking back, Tammy gives me the finger. Everything looks damp in the moonlight and the plastic glow of the street lamps. I think of leaving Rachel's house the night of our kiss and stopping to look in on Macy, half-covered, immaculately restful. A Popeye night-light in the wall. I touched her back and could feel her heartbeat. Her body was soft with sleep and her eyes were closed, lids trembling, knowing, even in her sleep and dreams, that her mother would come.

I can hear the party before I get there, music rolling out into the street. Gin's silhouette dances past the window holding a glass in either hand. The steaks are in a plastic grocery bag that swings against my leg when I walk. I just knock and open the door and someone says, "The meat is here."

"What's that supposed to mean?" I say.

Gin puts her arm carefully around my neck, holding her hand away because of the glass, and kisses my cheek. The Widow is on the couch, shoeless, ankles crossed, in sheer black stockings and a skirt. Ashlynn takes the steaks into the kitchen, her hair, down tonight but crinkled a bit from today's braid, floating out behind her, and returns with a glass of wine for me.

"We were just talking about you," she says. "When you were arrested for writing a bad check and all of us went down there to get you."

"You looked so pathetic in those little jail-issue flip-flops," the Widow interrupts, starting to laugh again. Obviously, they have already been laughing about this.

"And Gin started crying when she saw you looking all hangdog," Ashlynn says.

"The single worst day of my life," I say.

Candles are burning in the place of electric light. There are maybe twenty of them, the thick, cylindrical kind, some white, some cream-colored, sitting in saucers. They smell good. A small fish tank is bubbling on the mantle, and I walk over and tap the glass. There are two fish and they swim up to the side.

"I need to find you all something else to talk about," I say, grinning, pleased.

"But sweet little thang," Gin says, "you're my pride and joy."

"That's a song," I say.

"Sit down, cowboy," she says, pushing me into an armchair. We sit around the coffee table and eat the Gouda and crackers that Widow Friar has brought and pass the bottle of wine. Ashlynn has to go to the kitchen for another bottle. I ask where Rachel is and am answered with a community shrug and the talk turns back to their children and to movies and to me. I have been present for these talks before, their voices rising, quickening with excitement, as if telling secrets, as if discussing news from another planet. Paul has been fighting at day care. Gin tells us this with an undertone of pride.

He has, it seems, been winning. Tammy has been caught smoking. The Wolfe twins, Ashlynn's girls, who are eight and a half, are perfect angels, the Widow says, when compared with Tammy. A certain male heartthrob is playing a vampire in his new movie and everyone is worried about covering him with makeup for the part.

"I don't go to the show to see him act," Gin says.

"Or for the Milk Duds, if you know what I mean," Ashlynn says. She does a Groucho Marx cigar-tapping gesture at the corner of her mouth.

I just sit and listen and laugh and drink the wine that is poured into my glass. The candlelight is waving on the walls. Gin is sitting on the arm of my chair with her arm around my shoulders, occasionally letting her fingers comb through my hair, not thinking, the way I have seen her do for Paul when he is pressed shyly against her legs and she is talking to someone else. I tell them that I think the heartthrob is just a pretty boy and they say, what the hell do you think we've been talking about here. I tell them that I think it would be nice to have children and Widow Friar says, you can have mine, and then everyone chimes in laughing, take mine, take mine.

The door swings open and Rachel comes inside with Richard Davies. He is smiling and waving and looking a little lost. He is overdressed in a sport coat and tie but he looks good. I say, "Richard, what are you doing here?"

"Well," he says, "I asked Rachel to dinner and she said I should just come along with you guys."

"I hope it's all right," Rachel says. "I brought an extra potato. It was sort of last minute." She holds up a foil-covered tray of what I suspect is stuffed baked potatoes.

She does introductions. Everyone straightens up for the new arrival, standing, smoothing skirts and hair, assuring Rachel that, of course, he is welcome. Gin takes the tray from Rachel and whispers something in her ear.

"I think Rachel felt she needed some protection from me," Richard says.

"You're the one that needs protecting around here," Gin says over her shoulder, disappearing into the kitchen.

Widow Friar says, "We were just about to tell some more Wiley stories. You're not a Latin teacher, too, are you?"

"As they say in Rome," he says, smiling at me, "not if my life depended on it."

I follow Gin into the kitchen, carrying the wine with me. She is sliding the potatoes into the oven, the hot red light from the stove glowing on her face. There are no electric lights on in the kitchen either. I finish my wine, refill the glass, finish it again quickly, and pour another. The drinking makes my face warm.

"Ride 'em, buckaroo," Gin says, wagging a finger at my glass.

"Buckaroo?"

"That's my motif for the night. Wild West," she says. "See?" She puts one foot forward, heel on the ground, toe up, to show me her brown suede cowboy boots. Her jeans are tucked into them. She totters a little with all her weight on one leg and grabs my shirtsleeve for balance.

I take the wine and the steaks and carry them into the backyard. Someone has already started the grill and I pass my hand over the surface to check the temperature. The steaks hiss one by one as I lay them on the grill, drawing little tips of flame up from the charcoal. Inside, Richard was telling a story about when he used to counsel at a juvenile prison. Apparently, there was a young girl, sixteen, who was continually escaping, because her boyfriend said that if she didn't get out and come back to him, he would come over the wall and kill her. Each time she escaped and was brought back her sentence was extended, and each time her sentence was extended she tried to escape. They finally had to send her to an adult facility.

Richard said, "Actually she was a pretty nice girl but that's not the kind of love I want to fall in." Everyone laughed, even me.

"Hey there," Richard says behind me, startling me. He sits on the bench of a red cedar picnic table. Somewhere, I can hear a dog barking and rattling a fence.

"Nice ladies," he says.

"I'm glad you finally got to meet everybody," I say. "You'll have to come over later and see my place."

He looks over his shoulder to check the door and looks back, grinning wildly, rubbing his palms together. "Actually, your place isn't where I hope to end up later. Look out behind you," he says, pointing.

Flames are jumping up around two steaks and I pour a little wine on them. I offer him the bottle but he waves it off. A car door closes on another street, an engine starts. The patio is littered with leaves and they crunch under my feet.

"Tonight's the night with Rachel," he says. "I can feel it in my bones."

"Good luck, I guess."

"Have you got something going with one of them?" he says. "No, wait. Let me guess. Is it Gin? She's a sexy one."

I don't answer. I am suddenly angry at him. The music from the house stops, and we face each other, quiet, then it comes back on.

"Play nice," I say.

Richard looks at me like I've lost my mind.

"You bet." He stands and goes back inside.

I knock back my wine and wipe my mouth with my sleeve. I toss the glass hard against the back fence, but it doesn't break, just hits the chain link, bouncing end over end, and settles on the grass. The glass is rimmed with moonlight and raised slightly by the stiff blades of grass, held up like a gift offered on a satin pillow.

When I go back inside everyone is laughing. Richard waves his arms at me, for a moment laughing too hard to speak.

"Wiley, Wiley, thank God you're here," he says. "I need help desperately."

He is sitting in one of the armchairs, and Rachel is standing behind him, wearing his sport coat.

"Tell these ladies that gay men are sex fiends," he says.

"Sure they are." I shrug, play along.

"Baloney. They fall in love like everybody else. Why would they be hornier than regular couples?" the Widow says.

"They're both men," Gin says. Then to Richard, "You've spilled some wine on your tie. Take that thing off and let me get something on it before the stain sets."

She begins to unknot his tie, but he pushes her hands away and she straightens up, hands on her hips, like she's faced with a stubborn eight-year-old.

"I'm trained in psychology," Richard says, pulling his tie through his collar and handing it to Gin. He looks around her hip at us. "I've seen a lot of those boys and I'm saying some of the sweetest ones could suck a golf ball through a garden hose."

Ashlynn says, "What does that tell us about you, Richard?"

We all laugh, and Richard goes red in the face. I take two or three gulps from the bottle and hold it out to the room, offering it. Rachel says, "There's the other bottle. We have discovered the culprit."

I lean against the door frame and lick my lips. Wine makes me sleepy so I can never tell if I'm drunk. Everyone is watching me, even, I think, the fish, bumping up against the glass on my side of the tank.

"Easy on the vino," Gin says.

"In vino veritas," I say.

"I've got to get this tie," she says, taking the bottle on her way to the kitchen.

Richard says, "I never let your secret out about the wine."

Rachel's hand is on his shoulder, and he reaches his fingers up, drowsily, absentmindedly, to find hers. Right at that moment, seeing the way their fingers thread together, so naturally that neither of them seems to notice the gesture, I know that they are going to make love.

I creep up behind Gin in the kitchen, sweeping her hair aside with one hand, and kiss her neck. She is at the sink dabbing club soda on Richard's tie. The faucet is running. My other hand is curved around her belly, fingers at her middle. She pats my cheek. Her stomach is soft, and she smells of soap and shampoo. I kiss her again, behind the ear and turn her to face me. The room is dark except for a block of wavery light falling through the doorway. I hear Richard laughing in the other room. Gin rests her hand on my chest, wetting my shirt with her fingertips and she smiles sweetly. I kiss her on the lips, leaning into her, and for an instant, she is kissing back but she turns her head, straining her chin away from me, so I kiss her cheek, her throat, her eyes, pushing my legs against hers, mashing our chests together. She twists away, out from under my arms, and leaves me panting, bracing myself against the sink.

"Whoa, horse. That's it," she says. She is breathing hard as well, angry, one hand, palm up, between us in the air, like she is trying to stop traffic.

I go outside and flip the steaks but after the first three, I stop. They are black and ruined on one side, still blood red on the other. All of this shouldn't upset me so much. It is a wonderful night. To-day's clouds have all broken up, leaving the sky empty but for scat-tered stars and a huge cue-ball moon. The air is cool and pleasant. But I can't stop picturing Richard and Rachel together with Macy asleep in the next room or Macy barefooting down the hall to stand in her mother's doorway, the door left open in case she cried in the night. Even so, she isn't my daughter. I have no blood ties with these women or their children. I should put everything, all of this, out of my mind.

The house next to Gin's is vacant and the grass in the backyard is knee high. Beyond that, over a chain link fence, is Rachel's house and I can see from here that the TV is on, flicking blue light against the sliding glass doors that face the backyard. I go over the fence smoothly, through the grass without making a sound, and over the other side into Rachel's yard. The sliding glass door is locked. Tammy is asleep on the couch in front of the television. I circle the house, trying windows until I find one that is unlocked at Rachel's bedroom.

As I'm crawling through, my ankle gets caught in something, the phone cord, and I lose my balance and the phone and I go crashing to the floor. I lie perfectly still, not even breathing, listening for signs of life from the other room. I can barely hear the dial tone, then the operator telling me to please hang up, and over both of those, voices and distant applause from the television. But no Tammy.

I stand and tiptoe down the hall to Macy's room. She is sleeping on her stomach, one hand on the pillow next to her, her fingers curled under. Her lips are parted slightly. I bend and lift her from the bed, over the guardrail her mother has attached. She whines a little and twists in my hands but gives up quickly and settles against my chest, her head and smooth hair against my cheek. She is so warm. Nothing is as warm, almost feverish, as a sleeping child.

"Shhh," I say. "Hush now, Macy, baby. It's just me," and I walk her over to the window bouncing her a little on my toes, as I have seen mothers do. I don't know if Macy is too old for that but it doesn't matter. She turns her head and breathes on my neck.

I stand there for a long time, holding her, turning my hips slowly back and forth, looking at nothing in the backyard. A coiled garden hose. A red plastic child-sized football. Pine cones. I listen, trying to hear past the TV and the house creaking and settling its weight, for someone calling my name but no one is looking for me. Way off, lightly, I can hear a siren, flaring up and fading quickly, never coming close. The thing that I can't stop hearing is Macy's breathing, her and the night breathing, as gentle and sure as anything in the world.

Rachel will be home soon, probably with Richard. I lift Macy up, holding her at arm's length in the soft gray light, that curious light that you can only see at night. A combination of weak lights. She is almost weightless in my hands, just the barest pressure on my palms and wrists.

Her eyes are closed, her head lolling forward, and I shake her gently to wake her. I feel like I should tell her something, something important, but I can't think of anything. I try to remember all of the things my mother and father told me. Nothing seems to fit. In a minute or two, I will put her back into bed and leave the house the way I came in and no one, not even Macy, will know that I was here. She will think that she was dreaming. But maybe, if I can muster the right words, some of the dream will stay with her. I want to tell her something that only I know, that only I, of all people on earth, could possibly explain.

I think to tell her about love, what little I know of it, but I understand, there with the moonlight lying between us, that she doesn't need to be told. It is in her blood and touch and dreams, perfect and pure as an angel's wing.

Macy looks at me expectantly, a little confused but her face calm, eyes open wide. I remember, suddenly, what Solon told Croesus, the story that I told my class. Every day brings the possibility of change. You can't judge a man's happiness until he is dead.

I start to tell this to Macy but she draws in a breath, as if she is going to speak. She doesn't say anything, just holds it for a moment, her face ashen and smooth in the light, and lets it out with a patient sigh, a thing so adult, so beautiful, I nearly let her fall. All at once my arms are full of sand, and I pull her to my chest and hold her tightly against me. She is so small. She doesn't know anything. She doesn't even know enough to have dreams that won't come true.

"Just sleep," I tell her. That is enough for now.

Tenant

My landlady died in the fire that consumed her house, but the rescue squad was able to pull her unconscious dog, Shiloh, out of the flames and breathe life back into him. They revived him by wrapping a hand around his muzzle to keep it closed and huffing air into his nose. He woke—I am told; I was passed out drunk at the time—coughing up smoke like an old man. I live in an old slave cottage behind the main house that Mrs. Cunningham restored for renters. One of the firemen roused me some time later and I stumbled out onto the lawn in my underwear, already hung over. The fire was nearly out and the house was soaked and shadowy in the darkness, a faint mist rising from the walls and tiny, still burning embers winking in the wasted frame like cigarettes.

Shiloh was an enormous German shepherd, who relished tipping my trash cans and who couldn't get past his genetic predisposition for shepherding. Each day when I returned from work he met me at the car, determined to prevent me from reaching my front door. He circled me growling, rushed to block my passage, cut me into ever-shrinking corners. Charlotte, the woman I'd been seeing, was terrified of him and, in her defense, he did have forty pounds on her. He was big enough, upright, to pin my shoulders to the car with his paws and look me in the eye. I complained when I first moved to the farm, when Mrs. Cunningham was still alive, but she was at least seventy-five and could no more control Shiloh than I. She would grin and shake her head, as if he were a beloved only child and she found his bad habits endearing. I couldn't bring myself to demand that she leave the flower garden, where she spent her mornings, to collect the trash that was scattered in my yard. The very thought of a woman her age stooping to retrieve a paper plate made me shiver with guilt. Charlotte called the mess my own little garden, a lawn of perennials, she said, coffee filter buds, planted in TV dinner cartons, blooming each morning on liquor bottle stems.

When the policeman in charge of the fire scene had finished questioning me—Had I seen anything suspicious? No. Did I know Mrs. Cunningham to be unhappy? I did not—I called Charlotte. She had stayed home to study for the test I was giving the next day. I teach history at the little college in town. Charlotte was what the college calls a "continuing education" student, so she was in my class though she was four years my senior, a fact that did not exempt our relationship from the college's strict noninvolvement policy. She skipped college the first time around to try her hand at acting in Los Angeles but told me that all she did out West was hone her waitressing skills.

She was sleeping when I called but came out anyway, and we stood at my window, watching sirens flashing silently, men with smudged faces moving through the pinkish light in wet raincoats. Mrs. Cunningham's house was built in 1827 in the Tuscan style, a stucco Italian villa dropped into the middle of Alabama, complete with terra-cotta shingles on the roof and marble floors. That house and the 650 acres that surrounded it were the reasons I moved out there. I would have slept in a tool shed to live in its shadow. Burned now, blackened and crumbling in places, it looked like something from the ruins of ancient Rome.

"She was in the house?" Charlotte whispered, tapping the windowpane. We couldn't stop ourselves from whispering. She had come in a hurry and her hair was still mussed from sleeping and the pillow had drawn graceful lines on her face. I gave her a solemn nod.

Mrs. Cunningham had lived alone in the big house, the sole occupant of its thirty-two rooms, and didn't get out much, except to tend the garden. It was impossible to imagine Mrs. Cunningham as a young woman. My clearest memory was of her in the garden wearing a wide-brimmed straw hat to keep off the sun and long baby blue formal gloves, the sort women used to wear to balls. To protect her skin, she said. Despite her age, her hair was still faintly red and the hat pushed brittle rings of it down around her face. Occasionally, she asked me to come over to the main house and help her move a piece of furniture or lift a heavy box down from the attic. Mrs. Cunningham believed that, because I taught at the college, I must therefore be an intellectual, so when I was finished with her heavy work, she would have a question ready for me, along with a glass of iced tea. How close did we—she said we, as if she were there—really come to securing foreign intervention in the Civil War? How did I think history would view George Wallace? Her tone was always serious so I told her whatever I knew on the subject, sometimes shamefully little. We never talked about ourselves.

Around her, Shiloh was a different dog, docile but alert, curling at her feet beneath the kitchen table, growling if he thought I got too close. I think Mrs. Cunningham liked having a man on the property, but I may be flattering myself. My visits were infrequent. We rarely saw each other, though we lived not a hundred yards apart.

My cottage was situated in a grove of maples, and Charlotte and I would scare ourselves at night by pretending that the wind was slave voices singing old spirituals. We would sit under the dark trees and convince ourselves that we could almost make out the words. Neither of us believed in ghosts, so we weren't really afraid, just thrilled, like children telling stories, and we would go rushing back inside and build a fire in the huge stone hearth and heap blankets on top of the bed. The fear, even make-believe, added something to our lovemaking. My cottage was really just one big room with a shotgun kitchen and a sleeping loft beneath a cathedral ceiling, that drew the dancing, ghostly shadows away from us, leaving the rest of the room in warm brown light, like the light from a dream. We would stay that way, breathless and delightfully alone, the covers thrown aside now, the sheets sticking to our backs, until we heard Mrs. Cunningham calling Shiloh in for the night, her voice rising and falling, holding on the "shy" a few beats, then dropping off on "low." She would call maybe a dozen times, and we would hear her door close, and the house lights would begin to go off, one by one, leaving the yard in darkness.

The night of the fire, we watched the firemen collecting their gear, rolling thick black hoses, sheathing extension ladders. When the last of the trucks had gone blinking sadly down the driveway, Charlotte said, "I think I wanna see it. Let's examine the wreckage." She was already heading for the door.

"That's not a good idea," I said.

"Why not?" she said. "Why are we whispering?"

I didn't have an answer for her right then, so I caught her by the belt and hauled her into my arms, hoping that maybe I could get her into my bed and keep her away from Mrs. Cunningham's house. She took an imaginary pen and paper in her hands and read along as she wrote, "Dear Mr. College President, one of your professors, a certain Parson Price, has been making sexual advances toward me and I'm beginning to feel an uncomfortable pressure in class." She twisted free of my embrace and was out the door, marching across the lawn toward the house before I could stop her. There was no stopping Charlotte once she set her mind.

I jogged after her. We climbed through a section of collapsed wall and moved through the rooms downstairs, through burned-out doorways like cave mouths. Water was puddled on the floor. Somber smears of smoke streaked the walls. The fire started on the second floor, according to the fireman who woke me, and Mrs. Cunningham died in bed. We didn't go upstairs. Portions of the house were strangely undamaged, small surviving corners, where a lamp stood untouched, as if Mrs. Cunningham had just stepped out and might at any minute return and require a little light for reading. Being in the house felt wrong, like trespassing on something sacred.

Shiloh was around there somewhere. He didn't try to prevent us from entering, wouldn't even come near us, as if he understood that something dire had happened. Every now and then, we would see him slip past a doorway, wraithlike. It amazed me that something that big could move so silently.

"It's beautiful," Charlotte said. "In an awful way. It's more beautiful now than it was before, I think. It's less perfect, you know what I mean? It's like looking at someone's X-ray."

She stopped to examine a rosewood dining table, running her fingers along its dusty surface. Faint blue moonlight slanted in through window frames—the heat had caused the glass to explode outward—and through holes in the ceiling, where the second floor had burned. The light caught in the clean streaks left on the table by Charlotte's fingers.

"Someone died here tonight, Charlotte," I said. "We shouldn't be here."

"She *lived* here, too, Parson, for a long time. That's what's so amazing. Think of everything that happened here before you came along." Charlotte pressed her palm flat against the dining room wall. "Put your hand here," she said. "It's still warm."

"One of the guys from the fire department told me they think she started the fire herself. On purpose," I said.

Charlotte jerked her hand away from the wall.

"She wanted to kill herself?"

I told her what the fireman had told me. That the bedroom door was closed and locked but all the doors downstairs were open to whatever sort of intruder might want to help himself. The theory was that she wanted to bar Shiloh from the bedroom and be certain he had a way out of the fire. While I was talking, I watched Charlotte for a reaction. She walked over to the window, her steps crunching on the cooled embers that had rained down from upstairs. She stood there, perfectly still, and looked out at the night. A breeze moved past her and I could smell her perfume mixed in with the scent of ash. The moonlight was gauzy on her cheeks.

"You told me they had to carry Shiloh out of the fire," she said, turning toward me, her face now shadowed.

"Maybe he's too stupid to know that fire is a bad thing," I said.

"Maybe he didn't want to leave her." She faced the window again and cocked her head as if listening intently. I tried to hear what she was hearing. Cicadas ringing in the darkness. A train rumbling along the tracks that divided Mrs. Cunningham's property, just barely shaking the ground. Nothing much but those strange country sounds that only make you more aware of the silence behind them. Charlotte said, "That's the saddest thing I ever heard," and I didn't know whether she meant the plaintive night sounds or what I had just finished telling her.

I was a quiet tenant and, until Charlotte, had never brought a woman to the farm, so most of the complaints between Mrs. Cunningham and me tended to be mine, regarding Shiloh. I drink too much and would occasionally wander the fields at night. I don't know if Mrs. Cunningham was ever aware of my roving, though I have heard that old people tend to be light sleepers. She anyways never mentioned it, and I had lived on her farm for two years before she died. I would wander down to the railroad tracks or to watch the bats swarming over the pond, skimming for insects that lit on the surface. You could throw a stone out over the water and the bats would dive-bomb it, kamikaze runs, plunging themselves into the pond, blind by nature, stupid from hunger, after what they thought was food. It was a mistake, the first time I fooled the bats. I was just skipping rocks. The second stone was a test case to make sure the first wasn't a fluke or a figment of my imagination. After that, I tell myself that I was drunk, that I wouldn't have gone on tricking the bats with stones, if I had been sober. But I remember the buzz of power that came with killing without laying a hand, that came at the moment of impact, when a bat flashed through the night haze and smacked the surface, a sound like surprise, and didn't come up.

When we first started seeing each other, Charlotte asked me to tell her the worst thing I had ever done. She wanted to know how low I could go. She wanted to prepare herself for the worst. I thought about it for a while, then took her down to the pond and told her about the bats. She didn't say anything for a long moment, just looked at me, considering. I shifted awkwardly in her gaze, worried that telling her had been a mistake, that I had let her look into my thoughts and she had seen something too awful to stay. The bats slapped the air above us with their wings. Charlotte turned away from me to watch them. Her hands were in the pockets of her jeans and the wind was blowing, making her cheeks red, whipping her hair around her face, causing strands of it to stick to her lips. Softly, she said, "They're just bats." Then, turning back to me, smiling a little, gathering momentum, "They're blood suckers. Wait till deer season and look around for the blaze orange caps. Those are the nut jobs. Don't turn your back on those fuckers." I didn't know if she meant what she said, but I had never been more grateful.

There had been other women in my life during my time at Mrs. Cunningham's farm but only short-term, a weekend or two, and none of them had been invited to visit. The cottage was mine alone before Charlotte came along. She told me that she had been by herself a while, too, hadn't really felt at home with a man, until she stayed at my house. I can't speak for Charlotte, but I should say that I have always had trouble getting involved. In anything. I tried newspaper reporting after graduate school but couldn't get over the feeling that my work, even when writing the most innocent of stories, birth or wedding announcements, was an invasion of privacy. I wasn't long with the newspaper. I returned to history, for which I was originally trained. The stories of history had already been written.

The first night Charlotte spent with me was an accident of sorts. I had asked my students out to the farm for a get-acquainted picnic.

Both of us were drunk, inspired, I think, by the rest of the students, most of whom were underage. Charlotte stayed late to help me clean. Just before we went to bed, she said to me, "You think too much. You're educated to within an inch of your life, aren't you?"

Maybe so. Charlotte believed I was laughably careful about hiding our relationship from the administration. I passed her in the hall without speaking, called her by her last name in class. Probably, she was right, nothing would have happened if we were discovered. But I hated the "probably," hated its lack of guarantee. So she smiled indulgently to ease my apprehensions and promised again that she had told no one, that she would not ever tell.

We had the farm to ourselves for almost a month after the fire. Charlotte came out on the nights when she didn't draw the late shift at the Italian restaurant where she worked. Shiloh still frightened Charlotte, but she had softened toward him since hearing of his loyalty to Mrs. Cunningham. We took to leaving bowls of food for him, raw eggs cracked over white bread, leftover grits, on what used to be the patio of the main house. Charlotte believed we could win him over. I told her that I had tried bribing him before without success, but she thought that maybe Mrs. Cunningham's death had changed the dynamic between us.

Shiloh's enthusiasm for harassing me was beginning to flag and we felt sorry for him. At Charlotte's request, I made myself an easy target. We thought it might cheer him up. I would walk slowly around the main house, wear a groove back and forth to my car, but he didn't take advantage of my vulnerability. My path took me down to the pond, where a family of geese would scatter at my approach, and the stillness of the water was broken occasionally by a jumping bass. I even stood too close to the edge with my back to Shiloh, which I thought would be irresistible. He would keep me in sight but never come close, breeze through the high grass on my flank or stretch out on the hilltop above the pond, looking down on me, scrunch-eyed and serious like I was an algebra problem to be solved. I have to admit that there was something lovely about the way he moved, something

elemental, long and low to the ground. Once, when I had lost hope of
an attack, he hit me hard from behind. I sprawled on the grass trying
to catch my breath, and he curled up a few yards away. I had the feeling that he knocked me down for old times' sake.

When the sun was almost all the way gone, Charlotte and I would
drag my rocking chairs with the cane bottoms out onto the grass beneath the maples. It was warm for that early in the spring, but it was
cooler on the lawn than it was in my cottage. We played at being rich
on Mrs. Cunningham's farm. It was easy with the main house so
close, even a charred shell of it, easier now that Mrs. Cunningham
was gone. We could be her secret heirs. We debated putting in a
swimming pool.

"It'll be a godsend in summer," Charlotte said. "We could put it
right here under the trees and the branches would catch the pool
lights at night."

"But, Charlotte, this isn't Las Vegas," I said. "A pool just wouldn't
sit right."

We sat quietly a moment, considering the options. Charlotte said,
"We'll never come to an agreement, my love. Ask Montague to break
the tie." Montague was our imaginary butler. We laughed at our silli-
ness. We called each other "my love" and felt very English and, when
Charlotte asked for another glass of Dom Perignon, I knew that she
was referring to our bottle of grocery store wine. It seemed those
nights, my thoughts pretty with wine, that everything, the house, the
pond, the grand evening shadows that lingered on the lawn, that all
of this belonged to me.

Mornings, before my afternoons courting Shiloh and evenings
with Charlotte, belonged, however, to the college. Each spring, the
college cooked up some historical anniversary and served it to the
students in a section called "Topical History," taught by the low man
on the tenure ladder and monitored closely by the promotion committee. The class that fell to me was the fiftieth anniversary of both
VE and VJ day. I told my students about the U.S.S. *Indianapolis,* the
cruiser that delivered the atomic bombs to Okinawa so that they

could be dropped more conveniently elsewhere in Japan. On its return voyage, the *Indianapolis* was torpedoed and its crew set adrift on life rafts.

The class was interested that day, a detail I hoped wasn't lost on the committee observer. They are always interested when the subject is sex or death. I told them that the crew watched 80 percent of their shipmates be devoured by sharks, that many of them committed suicide, shot themselves, or gave themselves up to drowning, slipping their life jackets over their heads and letting the weight of their clothes drag them under. It was in their power to kill themselves. The sharks were beyond their control. One of the young men in class, a punk kid who always wore a black leather jacket embroidered with delicate chains and had f-u-c-k tattooed on the knuckles of his left hand and t-h-i-s on his right, and who was not at all impressed with me, asked, "What are we supposed to understand from that story?" This kid didn't like the grades I'd been giving him and had a knack for flustering me.

That night, Charlotte and I walked down to the pond and she said, "Every action has a consequence, my love."

The bats darted above us, their motion spastic and somehow too quick. I wouldn't have tricked them, but I looked for stones anyway. I liked the cold feel of them in my palm.

"That's what you should have told that student today," she said. "That's what he should have understood from the story of the *Indianapolis*."

"That's a rather occult revisionist take," I said. "I'm not qualified to teach karmic retribution. You might try Eastern Religions."

I played the moment over in my head, the question, my embarrassed stuttering and note shuffling, like I had the answer written down right there if I could only find it, the committee observer watching all of this. What I came up with in class, after considerable flailing, was, "There's nothing to understand *per se*. It's just a story. Something interesting and terrible that happened once. Something that bears remembering."

*   *   *

We had several visitors to the farm after the fire. An insurance agent taking Polaroids, then an artist who wanted to paint the ruined house. Shiloh greeted each visitor ferociously, chasing them back to their cars and pressing his muzzle to the window, foaming on the glass. I would leave whatever I was doing and cross the lawn from my cottage, a toothless dog, to inspect the stranger, to bestow or withhold my approval like the lord of the manor. One evening, about a month after Mrs. Cunningham's death, we heard Shiloh barking, then a woman's voice dismissing him, "Quiet, dog. Lay one paw on me and you're history," and before I could leave my chair to reconnoiter, she rapped once on the door and let herself in without waiting for an invitation. "You're Parson Banks," she said. "I'm Brady Cunningham. Your landlady's daughter."

I hadn't even realized that Mrs. Cunningham had children. I had imagined for her a spinster's existence with maybe a lover lost at sea or leaving her at the altar. But here was this woman, small and wiry like Mrs. Cunningham, with Mrs. Cunningham's red hair, standing in my cottage, one hand still loosely on the doorknob, claiming to be her child and informing me that they were putting the property on the market. "Don't get up. I just thought you should know," she said. "As eldest daughter, I'm serving as executrix for the estate. I've got a sister who isn't altogether happy with me in charge, but the one thing we can agree on is to get rid of this old place. It's a financial sinkhole."

Two children, daughters. Charlotte was in the kitchen cracking raw eggs into a bowl for Shiloh, when Brady came in, and she stayed there, silent, her hands poised over the bowl, fingers dripping yolk. This daughter was all business, telling me that the cottage was still mine, until they found a buyer. I would pay my rent to an estate account. She wasn't interested in my sympathy. When I said, "I'm sorry for your loss," she said, "Don't be. I haven't spoken to that woman in almost ten years. Mother was the meanest woman I ever knew."

She stepped backward out of the house, closed the door behind her, opened it again, and leaned inside. She said, "Oh, and if you see my sister around here trying to take anything out of the house, call the police. She looks like me only blonder and taller." Before I could tell her that I didn't want to get involved, didn't want to be in the middle of an inheritance dispute, she was gone, the door shut firmly between us. I heard Shiloh barking again, then her car heading off, tires crunching on the gravel driveway. I hadn't left my chair. Wind rustled in the chimney. I turned to face Charlotte and raised my eyebrows in a question. She said, "Don't ask me what that was all about. Who does she think she is barging in here? You tell me that. Her mother's dead a month before she decides to show her face. And then only to sell the house. Her mother's house, Parson." We looked at each other a moment longer before Charlotte went back to cracking eggs.

Brady Cunningham didn't bother to do anything about Shiloh. A For Sale sign appeared at the end of the driveway a few days after she left, but I pulled it out of the ground and tossed it into the rain gully beside the road so it would look like it had been knocked over accidentally. A realtor began stopping by to show the house. Because of the fire, it was a bargain basement deal. Most of the potential buyers were nice enough, assuring me that if they decided to purchase the place I would be able to stay on as a tenant. They were wealthy people from out of state, looking for a lifestyle change. I hated that word, lifestyle. There was an oilman from Texas, a computer genius, close to my age but worth about a million times as much, even a movie actress whose stardom was beginning to fade. Each of them asked me how I liked living on Mrs. Cunningham's farm. I didn't tell them that I would buy it in an instant, if that were within my means. When the realtor wasn't listening, I would invent reasons for them not to buy and offer them grudgingly as if I were just giving a little friendly advice. A fictitious article I had read about how expensive and ultimately impossible it was to restore fire-damaged houses to their original condition. The biblical swarms of biting insects that descended on the house at dusk or the plague of rats that infested the basement in winter. I found that the most effective technique was simply to rehash the details of Mrs. Cunningham's suicide. Often the realtor hadn't apprised them and I found that telling the story that way, adding my own specifics—Mrs. Cunningham soaking the bed and carpet in gasoline, before crawling under the covers with a match—her suicide began to seem like just another invention to prevent the house from being sold.

Brady Cunningham began coming out to the farm more often once the house was on the market. We'd see her from my porch in her bib overalls and work gloves, her hair tied back with a bandanna, Aunt Jemima–style. She would emerge from the house sooty and disheveled, carrying a cardboard box of salvageable goods. Every now and then, she gave us a smile or a tentative wave, which we vehemently ignored. Charlotte had an idea that Brady was somehow connected to her mother's death or, at least, that she knew something that she wasn't telling, and that in the boxes that she took away was the evidence. When she was gone, we would slip into the house and try to discern what was missing, but neither of us was familiar enough with the place to recognize an absence. We found gaps in the charred bookcase but couldn't remember what, if anything, had been there before. End tables with blank surfaces, empty drawers in which we could not find a clue. The only thing missing, that we could tell, was Mrs. Cunningham.

Shiloh stayed clear when Brady was around. Charlotte wondered why he didn't attack, why he didn't drive her screaming from the grounds. She worried that Brady Cunningham's appearance had somehow robbed him of his spirit. I said, "He's a dog, Charlotte. What you're saying implies that he understands what's happening around here." But I worried, too. Sometimes, when we went down to the main house to collect the bowls that we had left for him, we discovered the food eaten, sometimes not. I worried that Shiloh wasn't getting any of it, that a raccoon or something was reaping the rewards of my generosity. I decided to become a spy.

I set the food in plain sight and climbed the stairs to find a hiding place with a good vantage of the patio. The staircase had at one time been a wonderful thing, with a thick, smooth banister that curved down from the second floor like a graceful slide, but now its surface was charred rough and I was afraid to put weight against it for fear that it might collapse. I stepped gingerly in the darkness. Upstairs, in the hallway beside the master bedroom, I found a narrow break in the wall, where a section of mortar had come loose, thin like in a gunner's turret, that let through a rectangle of light. The moon was almost full and I could see, from my hiding place, the dark shape of the house spreading gently on the lawn, not moving when the breeze pushed through the high, uncut grass.

I watched the plate of food for hours, but nothing came to eat it. Most of the wall between my hiding place and the bedroom had burned away, and I could see the moonlight playing in there, too, casting strange shadows. Something caught my attention, a rustle, motion glimpsed out of the corner of my eye. I wasn't alone in the house. I held my breath and listened. Nothing. No sound but the night humming. I felt a presence though, like knowing someone is behind a tinted window, even though they can't be seen.

I whispered, "Shiloh, that you? You don't scare me, you punk dog. I wipe my ass on punks like you." Of course, there was no answer. I was spooking myself. I had to resist the temptation to look in Mrs. Cunningham's bedroom to make certain her body was gone. I had seen her bedroom once before the fire. She had asked me to carry a box of linens upstairs for her and I sat it down on the very bed in which she died. Arched windows paneled one wall and they were full of sunlight, which drifted inside and electrified motes of dust. Mrs. Cunningham came into the room behind me, carrying a smaller, lighter box, and I took it from her and held it while she caught her breath. She rested one hand softly on my arm, the other on her chest, and smiled apologetically. The meanest woman I ever knew, her daughter had said, but I couldn't see it. Mrs. Cunningham was already an old woman when I met her, so it was difficult, there in the cindery darkness of her house, to imagine her with enough passion in her to do something that would drive her daughters away, enough despair to choose this particular way of dying. I imagined I could smell gas very faintly when the breeze moved through the walls.

Charlotte insisted we start riding home from the college together. She said it was high time we stopped pretending. Time to take charge. "We'll do it on a Friday," she said. "Kick start the weekend." My heart pounded until we were well past the front gate, as if I were carrying drugs or the body of a murdered colleague in the trunk. Friday night, we grilled steaks under the waning moon and when we heard dogs barking in the distance, we joined them. We crouched on the ground and howled until our throats were sore. We made love in the high grass. The grass hadn't been cut since the fire and was full of spring wildflowers.

Later, Charlotte and I lay in bed naked, while I read over my lesson plan and Charlotte did her homework. The sheet was pulled up to our waists, so her chest was uncovered and I was having a little trouble concentrating. Charlotte looked up from her book and said, "If I die tomorrow—say I'm hit by a bus—how would you commit suicide?"

"Don't be morbid," I said.

"I would probably slit my wrists in the bathtub," she said. "Not over you, understand. I wouldn't be as devastated by your death as you would by mine." Here, she smiled and gave my hand a squeeze. "But if I had to commit suicide, razor blades and warm water would be the way to go."

"I'd eat a bullet," I said. "Quick and painless."

"Doesn't make for a handsome corpse though, does it?" Charlotte made a gun with her hand, put the index finger barrel between her lips, pulled the trigger, and collapsed dead with her head on my chest, her hair tickling my neck. She put her hand on my stomach and circled my belly button with her damp fingertip.

"What about hanging?" I pointed at the rafters. "Throw a rope up there and jump from the loft."

"Very romantic," she said. "But far more agonizing than a garden hose from the exhaust pipe."

"I've got it," I said. "Sleeping pills and booze."

She didn't answer. She drew in a breath and held it. Everything was quiet. The startled silence that follows a gunshot. I could feel her going still, softening against me, letting all the energy slip out of her muscles. I put my hand on her back. The only sign of life I could feel in her was her heartbeat, quickening each second she refused to breathe. I counted a hundred beats before she threw the covers back, exhaling, and put her feet on the floor, her back to me, the way a drunk steadies himself when the room spins. She lifted her hair away from the back of her neck. The underside of her hair was damp with sweat.

"What could have possibly made her want to die like that?" she said.

I scooted over on the bed and blew softly on her shoulders to cool her.

"She must have done something unspeakable," she said.

"I try not to think about it," I said.

"You must have thought about it."

Charlotte and I had been carpooling from campus for about a week, leaving the old brick buildings together and crossing the busy quadrangle to the parking lot, my worry easing gradually from me with each uneventful trip, when I received an anonymous message on my answering machine. "I know about your little secret," the voice said, "I know all about the teacher's pet." My skin inched along my bones. The voice was disguised, baritone, as if the speaker was young and imitating a grown man, but I would have sworn it was the kid with the leather jacket and tattoos. I played the message over for Charlotte a few times to confirm my suspicions about the identity of the speaker. She said, "Screw that little shit. You let me worry about him."

I discovered her by accident, a few days later, standing over him in the men's bathroom near my office. She must have tracked him to the spot, waited until she knew he would be alone. He was cowering in a corner and she had the collar of his jacket in one hand and a can of mace in the other. The kid was wearing some sort of kilt that day and black long underwear bottoms with his jacket and Doc Martens. He had his hands in front of his face, begging her not to spray him, and looked absolutely terrified. Neither of them heard me come in, and I slipped back into the hall and let the door swing quietly shut. I didn't want her to know that it frightened me to see her like that, full of violence and potent with ire. It excited me some as well. I didn't want to have to tell her that, despite my anger, I didn't think that I could do what she had done. From the kid, we never heard another word on the subject. I eased up a little after that, when I was grading his papers.

The computer genius bought Mrs. Cunningham's house in April. He came down to close the deal and told me that it would be eight months or so before the restoration was complete. He was a nice enough guy, with wire-rimmed glasses that kept slipping down the bridge of his nose. We had a few drinks—for a computer guy he could put it away—and he offered me a renewed lease and I accepted, pretending that I was grateful and that I was happy for him.

"You should buy," he said. "I don't want to sacrifice my tenant, but renting's a losing proposition. Land's the only real investment. Land and computers. This place is gold." I wanted to hit him right then, to warn him off somehow, as Charlotte had my student. He raised his drink in a toast to land and computers and brought it to his lips and knocked the edge against his glasses, spilling a little, bumping the glasses crooked. He blinked and straightened his glasses on his nose. Probably he had been one of those kids I used to feel sorry for when I was a kid myself, but who was sorry for who now? Apparently, Shiloh had done his shepherding routine on my new landlord the day he signed the papers. I apologized and told him that the dog belonged to me. I assured him that it wouldn't happen again.

When the construction crews began arriving, along with hordes of people from the historical society who took it upon themselves to make certain the rebuilding fit the original model, I began to see Shiloh less. He became nocturnal. I still don't know if he ate the food that I left out for him, and I hoped sometimes that he didn't, that he was feeding himself in the wild, not depending on anyone, gorging on rabbits and opossum that he hunted.

Charlotte and I would sit on the hill above the house, concealed by the high grass, and watch the construction crews at work, watch the men walk along the spine of the roof, like tightrope walkers, one foot on either side. When they had shut down the machinery and abandoned their equipment for the day, we would steal down to the site, furtive as Apaches, to inspect their progress. Where there had been charred plaster appeared new stud wall and reinforced support beams. They leveled ruined walls, chipped away damaged moldings, and brought in cement and sand and hydrated lime and laid new stucco over whatever masonry was salvageable. The stucco went on wet, glistened in the evening light. Charlotte leaned close to examine the faint, slightly discolored lines where the new walls met the old. She pressed the stucco with her thumb and it gave a little, allowed itself to be manipulated like putty, nearly hardened. She circled through the house, running her fingers along the walls, eyes narrow with apprehension, toeing piles of rubble and surveying the contents a little too closely, kneeling to examine the seams between blocks of new marble. I liked the way she looked with her hair pulled back, her eyes intent on her careful inspection.

Mounds of debris, ruined shingles and mortar, blackened pieces of the original frame, and chalky hunks of drywall, accumulated on the lawn and Charlotte couldn't stand the sight of them, so every once in a while, we hauled a load down to the railroad tracks to make a bonfire. A train would come rumbling by and the conductor would see our fire and blow his whistle. We stood close to the train to feel the wind in its wake, close enough that it became a passing blur, the lettering on the cars unreadable. We didn't say much. Most nights we were too tired to make love.

The fire made a genial orange circle in the clearing, sent up looping streams of sparks like fireflies. Shiloh would wander down to watch us and sit at the fringe of the light. Charlotte would whistle and call his name, trying to get him to join us in the firelight. He'd whine and pace back and forth in the shadows, as if he wanted to come closer but something was holding him back.

Brady Cunningham returned on a Saturday. Charlotte was working the day shift at the restaurant, and I was alone. I was grading papers and heard voices outside and went to the window to see who was trespassing on my property. Two women, one of them Brady, stalked circles around each other in the gravel behind the house. They were wearing similar black dresses and heels, both of them reddish blond, looking almost identical from a distance, and it occurred to me that there might have been some sort of memorial service that day and I wasn't invited, which made me a little angry. They were too far away for me to make out all of what they were saying, but I could catch snatches of name calling, and it was easy enough to hear the anger in their voices. Their movement was jerky and tense, like marionettes, and it seemed from my vantage point as if this whole thing wasn't real, was being staged for my benefit.

Brady turned suddenly and looked at my window. Her shoulders relaxed and she pushed her fingers through her hair. It was a moment before I realized she was looking at me, watching me watch them. She waved, and I threw myself prone on the floor beneath the window. When I had gathered the courage to look again, she was crossing the lawn to my cottage, wobbling a little when her heels sunk into the ground. I flopped down again and belly-crawled to the front door to lock it and then to the bathroom to hide. I was certain she was going to drag me into the middle of their argument somehow. I sat in the shower with the curtain pulled. I didn't move, even when she pounded on the door and circled the house trying windows, shouting, "I know you're in there. You aren't fooling anybody."

The longer I listened to her shouts and reproachful knocks, the more humiliated I became. I felt pathetic and weak, sitting there, damp from the shower floor, my arms circling my knees. She could outwait me. She knocked long enough that it became apparent that she wasn't going to leave. Eventually, I went slinking to the door, a beaten dog, and let her inside.

"I was in the bathroom," I said.

She waved my explanation away. Her eyes were red from crying, and she wanted to know if I had any gin. I watched her sister driving away in a humpbacked brown station wagon.

"I just wanted to take a last look at the place," Brady said.

I went inside and fixed us glasses of gin and grapefruit juice and brought them back out onto the porch. We made small talk—she was living in New Mexico; I was originally from Louisiana. I prepared a dozen statements in my mind to rebuke her for the way she had treated her mother in death. But I didn't say anything.

"Are you married?" she said.

"No. You?"

"Not me. Mother was married three times," she said, swirling her drink. She pressed her fingertips to her eyes. "Did you know that?"

"No." I did not. It occurred to me, then, not for the first time, that there were other things I didn't know. I had no idea what had happened between Brady and her mother. But something *had* happened. I was sure of that. And, all of a sudden, I didn't want to know what it was. I was afraid that she was going to tell me. It took me eight drinks to get through her visit. She kept talking, telling stories about her mother—Mrs. Cunningham had worked on an ocean liner, when she was young, had been in charge of teaching the passengers to hula dance; I couldn't believe it—but she never did tell me why she left. She stayed on my front porch long enough for night to settle on us and bring the fireflies out. There must have been a thousand of them, winking and twisting, leaving faint impressions of themselves on the darkness. I could see them in the most distant fields, adding depth, making the land look as big as the sky.

Brady said, "When I was a girl, I used to try and catch them in Mason jars with holes punched in the lids. Right out there. I had this idea that I could light my room with their tails."

"That's a nice memory," I said.

"It's one of those things," she said. "You don't even know you've forgotten it, until it's right there in front of you."

It was dark enough that I couldn't see her face.

"Do you want me to turn a light on?" I asked.

"No," she said. "Please don't."

I could tell that she was crying again.

The next day it rained and the construction crew didn't come. Charlotte arrived after work and we walked down to the driveway and sat in the cab of a hauling truck the crew had left behind. We watched the house through blooms of rain on the windshield. It felt like we were waiting for something. The keys were dangling from the ignition, so I gave them a half-turn to run the wipers and the radio. The only station we could get played country songs.

"Should we go in?" she said.

"I don't really feel like it," I said.

She didn't answer. The rain came down in fits and starts, one minute hard enough that our view was completely obscured, the next so gently that the wipers whined across the windshield. We saw Shiloh come up over a hill behind the pond and stand there looking down on everything. His fur was matted to his body with rain, showing clearly the weight he had lost, and he looked wolfish and severe. He trotted to the water's edge, padded in a circle, then curled up, throwing his tail over his nose.

"I was wondering about a dog's memory," Charlotte said. "I've heard it's out of sight out of mind for dogs. They forget their owners, if they're separated for more than a couple of weeks."

"I think he remembers her," I said.

"What does he remember about her?"

"Her voice, her smell," I touched the keys, the rabbit's foot key chain. "He remembers the way she looked."

"What else?"

"You name it," I said. "He remembers everything."

The rain was coming down hard again and it was difficult to pick

Shiloh out in the high grass. Charlotte covered my hand, the one that was jangling the keys, with hers. I thought I was bothering her, that she was going to ask me to stop, but she didn't. She just sat there, looking out, touching my fingers.

That evening—the quiet and the rain, Charlotte's hand on mine—had a dusty feeling, was colored with the hazy light of something that had already happened. I didn't know, then, that the end for the two of us was already beginning. A second ticked by, and another and on and on, relegated by their passing to history, joining the long stream of time that already included Mrs. Cunningham's death and would eventually, after just a few more months of marking time, encompass the day that Charlotte would return to California to give acting another shot. She would leave before the house was finished, gleaming and perfect, as though it had never caught fire. And she would leave before Shiloh disappeared. I would begin to see him less and less as the house neared completion, and then, one morning, I would wake and walk outside to stand beneath the trees, and he would be gone. But I, of course, didn't know any of this then, sitting there with Charlotte in the fading rain. As we watched, bats began to materialize in the air above the pond as if from nowhere. Shiloh's head snapped up at the sound of them, their chirping, their fluttering wings. I wondered if it was true that he remembered everything about Mrs. Cunningham, even what it was that made him love her. Shiloh got to his feet and snapped at the bats that flew too near. He charged into the shallow water after them and they cartwheeled above him, frenzied by his pursuit. Shiloh rose up on his hind legs, still snapping, reaching higher, swatting with his paws, and for an instant, with Shiloh standing precariously and the bats whirling above him, it was as if they were performing an ancient ritual dance, as old and as candid as time. That I would remember. Shiloh dancing with the bats in the leathery twilight. I would make it mine.